Bloodlines

To Drink the Wind

Idella Washington Smith

authorHOUSE®

AuthorHouse™
1663 Liberty Drive
Bloomington, IN 47403
www.authorhouse.com
Phone: 1 (800) 839-8640

Published by AuthorHouse   01/22/2016

ISBN: 978-1-5049-6885-0 (sc)
ISBN: 978-1-5049-6884-3 (e)

Library of Congress Control Number: 2015920986

Print information available on the last page.

BLOODLINES

A synopsis

Adele

"To drink the wind" is a phrase often used to describe the running ability of Arabian race horses. Though Adele is an extremely accomplished young woman of twenty, she realizes that she's no thoroughbred debutante. She's an authoress/graduate student who dreams of "drinking the wind" just once with the arrogant and charismatic Jet, the man who owns the thoroughbred horse ranch where she's a parttime stablehand. She has put in motion a plan to seduce Jet. Despite all the obstacles that threaten her plan's success, Adele is intent on experiencing her one night of love with Jet in which she will live out her fantasies. Then she plans to get on with her life.

Jet

Jacque Entione Trideaux whose Creole bloodlines can be traced back over two hundred years wants to add new blood to his family dynasty. Though he is on the brink of becoming a billionaire, this long held ambition has taken second place to his heart's desire—Adele. He wants to be more than just the object of Adele's romantic fantasies. Beautiful, headstrong, and outrageously unpredictable, Adele affects him in a way no other woman ever has. Soon after Jet has decided to make Adele his wife and set forth a plan to train and mold her into becoming the kind of wife he needs, he learns a secret about her family history that makes the possibility of him marrying her almost nil to none.

The Story

Bloodlines is a fairytale with a contemporary twist. It introduces to the world of romance a delightful and fascinating heroine and hero—Adele and Jet. This story allows the reader to take a romantic journey that is fraught with tension and excitment and numerous instances of romantic love and sizzling passion.

PROLOGUE

"Where to boss?" What destination should I file on the flight plan? "The airplane pilot patiently waited for an answer from the man who was making green colored notations on a set of business papers that he was reading.

"Jacques Entoine Trideaux, Jet to most people, raised his eyes from the balance sheet he was analyzing and stared at his airplane pilot as if he was grappling with a difficult decision. Then his eyes fell on the pen that he was holding, an inexpensive gift that used a hundred dollar bill as its outer design. It was precious to him. A whimsical smile played at the corners of his mouth. The pen invariably had such an effect on him. It was a joke gift given to him by someone who was very special to him. A sudden light of certainty glowed in his dark eyes. He closed the pen with profound reverence, after all, he may have just signed the business deal of his lifetime with that pen. Jet flashed a decisive smile at his airplane pilot.

"St. Pierre, Louisiana in the U.S. of A. He drawled." "I'm going home, James."

It was the pilot's turn to look uncertain. "Not New Orleans, sir?" "No." Jet sighed. "I want to go home to St. Pierre." He was bone tired and he felt much older than his thirty-two years. "I've been away far longer than I intended." He sighed once more and added, "but it couldn't be helped and it was definitely worth it."

"Is this the deal, Mr. Trideaux, the one that will do it for you?" James asked.

"It just might be the one. If my JetStream automatic car washers are half as popular over here as they are back in the states, my corporate net worth should hit the magic mark before this years end."

"Well, I'll keep my fingers cross for you, sir."

Thanks, James I appreciate it." Jet studied James for a moment. "James, I believe you're as excited by the possiblity of my becoming billionaire as I am.

"That I am sir." Though we come from different sides ofthe creek, we are connected.

"Irrevocably." Jet agreed. "We're black men."

James chuckled. No, one would ever guess it by the looks of you." Your skin's lighter than those Japanese businessmen to whom you're selling franchises."

Jet chuckled softly. "Notwithstanding, I'm proud of who I am." Skin color doesn't matter.

"You've the first Creole I ever heard say that."

"Well, James you must haven't been around many Creoles."

"That's true. Never spent much time in New Orleans. Anyway, the ones that I have been around all wanted to pass as Spaniards or something." Didn't you guys use to have a brown paper bag test or something to determine if a person was light skinned enough to belong to you alls social clubs?

"Sadly, that was true in the past. "I admit some Creoles of the old thought are still like that." But most are like me, proud of their African ancestry."

James stuffed his hands in his pockets and looked sheepish. "I hope that I wasn't out ofline saying what I said."

"Don't fret over it. "I respect your candor."

As James turned to leave, Jet asked in a light tone, "can you sat this lady down safely on that small airfield?

The pilot flashed a self-assured smile before he answered. "Mr. Trideaux, you better than anyone, know that I can land this lady practically anywhere."

Jet was reflective for a moment. "Yes, I believe you can at that."

Once more, James turned to leave. Then he paused. "You know, Mr. Trideaux, now that you own your own private jet people will get even a bigger kick out of calling you by your nickname, Jet."

"I confess. That thought did occur to me." Jet let go of a mischievous laugh that almost erased the look of fatigue from his features. Then he queried, a teasing note in his tone, "don't you think it is about time you started calling me Jet as well?

"Will do sir . . ., I mean Jet." James flashed a slightly self-conscious smile and gave Jet a small salute—a habit he'd picked up during his stint in the Air Force. "My parents will get a kick out of seeing me land this lady. I'll call ahead later and let them know when we'll land."

"You do that James. Jet said distractedly as he accepted a chilled fruit drink from the co-pilot.

Long after James had returned to the cockpit to file a flight plan, Jet pondered the brief conversation he'd just shared with his pilot. "From different sides of the creek" was a gross understatement. James had grown up in poverty whereas he had grown up in the lap of luxury with all the benefits of a wealth grounded in banking and real estate. However, alone with the benefits came responsibilities. Quite often it seemed as if the responsibilities were greater than the wealth.

When he was just barely fifteen his childhood had ended abruptly when his father had died in an airplane crash while traveling with his mistress often years. Though the Trideaux wealth and power had been used to keep the scandal from becoming public knowledge, his mother and he had known. His mother had been crushed by his father's infidelity. So, he had taken on the responsibilities of protector of his mother's happiness and protector of the family's wealth. So far he done a pretty good job at both. By versifYing into such areas as manufacturing, offshore drilling, automatic carwashing, nightclubs and gambling casinos, he'd increased the Trideaux wealth of seven million to 700 million by the time he was thirty. At present, it had grown to about 890 million. Also, he had been a good son to his mother. These days she was happy as could be. She was the undisputed queen of Creole society in New Orleans. Her life was filled with elegant little Teas, social galas and large fundraising banquets. His success with money and his mother's well-being had come at a cost. By the time he was twenty-five, he had developed an ulcer and he'd become skeptical about whether or not he would find true love and happiness in life. However, four years later he had met someone whose presence in his life had improved the state of his ulcer and his state of skepticism about love and happiness. He'd met her in the most unlikely place, a grubby salvage yard.

The infamous red sunset of Japan glistened off the ebony wings ofthe corporate jet as James speared it toward the clouds. Jet leaned back in one of the custom made recliner seats of his 707 that he had renovated into a flying hotel. In recent months, it had became more expedient and perhaps necessary for him to own a corporate jet that was capable of international flights.

Jet touched a button on the arm of his seat. As the sound of Mozart floated about him, he closed his eyes and let the fatigue, he had been holding at bay by sheer will, washed over him. In about twelve hours they would be landing at Heathrow airport in England for rest and refueling.

From there they would fly nonstop to his small private airport at St. Pierre.

St. Pierre was a rural area about seventy miles northwest of New Orleans. He discovered the area four years earlier when he had been looking for a place to build a new plant. There he'd built a sprawling horse ranch in which he had named Fiveforks after the name of the river that dominated his land.

He was going home to Fiveforks and her. As he drifted off to sleep, a vision of soft brown eyes and rich brown skin the color of toasted almonds and as flawless as satin, played on his cognizance. "Adele". He mumbled before he fell into a deep sleep.

CHAPTER ONE

Powerful legs striving, straining forward, and then all four hooves were suspended in midair for a microsecond. Sangfroid was beauty to behold. It was springtime in St. Pierre and the horses were running at Fiveforks, Jacques Trideaux's two-thousand acre Arabian horse ranch. It was rural Louisiana at its most beautiful. The landscape of moss shrouded magnolia trees and majestic oaks along Fiveforks River provided the perfect backdrop for the beautiful horses. Sangfroid, the pride and joy of Fiveforks, was the most beautiful of all. He was a throughbred.

"He's flying." "Look at him fly." Oh, how he drinks the wind!" Adele squealed gleefully, almost losing her perched position atop the whitewashed board fence. And she would have, if a pair of strong hands hadn't steadied her. She didn't seem to notice.

Jet inhaled and took a deep breath of the crisp morning air. It was early April, and the mornings still had a bit of a chill in them. Adele's youthful exuberance never failed to take his breath away. God, how he loved her.

Adele was oblivious to the deep gaze of the tall man beside her. At that moment, she had eyes only for the beautiful animal that had just swished by.

"You broke yesterday's record didn't ya boy?" Adele yelled into the trail of flying dirt left by the magnificent beast.

"Let's check it out with Eddie." Jet suggested.

The warm cadence of Jacques Trideaux's deep Creole drawl flowed over her like an earthy blues melody and affected a tiny little shiver to run down her spine. And as usual Adele was consumed with a joy of just being near him. He was to her what Mark Anthony had been to Cleopatra—her hero, her passion, her fantasy.

"Well, we will know soon enough, Mr. Eddie is headed this way." Adele stammered. She was mesmerized by the way the golden rays of the morning sun glowed like honey on the Adonis that was standing so near her. Soon, he would be sporting a beautiful tan. Another tiny shiver of excitement ran down her spine.

"You're cold," Jet told her. He took off the denim jumper he was wearing and draped it about her shoulders." His kind gesture almost made Adele lose her place on the fence once more. This time she noticed when he kept her from falling. She prayed a fervent silent prayer that he wouldn't hear the way that her heart was pounding. What was wrong with her? Maybe it was because it was spring, and her blood like that of the beautiful horses bred on the ranch was set on fire by nature's promise of procreation. Whatever the reason, lately she had been consumed by the thought of Jet making love to her.

At that moment, she was fighting a strong urge to bury her face in Jets warm jacket and inhale deeply. Instead, she feigned an exaggerated concentration of the man that was walking, as fast as his squatty legs would carry him, toward them.

"Mr. Trideaux, you're not going to believe it, he cut off a whole five seconds from yesterday's run.' Eddie Thibodeaux, the horse trainer, was besides himself with joy and waving his stop watch wildly. At that moment, his complexion usually the color of an old penny was gleaming like one just from the mint.

"Yep, I do believe he's ready for his first professional race, Eddie." Jacques Trideaux turned to Adele at that moment. "I've entered Sang-froid in a race at Lincoln Downs next week and I want you to be there," he said, as matter of fact.

Jet words made Adele feel as if she was caught in a sudden storm whose winds would blow away everything that was familiar to her.

"Do you really mean that?" her voice quivered slightly, "You really mean to take me with you?"

"Yes, I do", Jet assured her, allowing an indulgent smile to play on his mouth and in his dark eyes.

"Really?"

"Yes," he assured her once more. And this time there was a note of laughter in his voice.

Adele was still afraid to believe. She risked looking into Jet's black eyes which she didn't do to often because there was always that possibility that she would get lost in their dark depths and never find her way out agam.

Jet was trying very hard to kept his voice even and his feelings for the young woman hidden. But that was almost an impossibility when she looked at him in that frighten yet provocative way that made him feel protective. He fought back an urge to throw his arms around her and tell her that he would never let anyone or anything hurt her, especially himself. Albeit, he couldn't. It was too soon.

Instead he said, "I believe you love that horse more than I do." He's your baby. It is only fitting that you be there for his first professional race." Still he struggled to keep his deep feelings for the girl from entering into his voice. But that was a difficult thing to do, when love for her withered and surged through ever fiber of his being and threatened to overflow like the serpentine Fiveforks River during the spring floods.

Eddie watched the exchange between his boss and the young woman. A glimmer of mischief added sparkle to his smoky gray eyes. He had been with Jacques Trideaux for a very long time. He knew the man almost as well as he knew horses. Jacques wasn't fooling him. Not at all. The man was a gonna for that lovely little filly of a gal.

"Well Eddie, what do you think?"

"Well, boss I think that ones a real winnah". He took his hat off for a moment and rubbed his head and glanced at Jet and Adele with a knowing glint in his eyes. Yep, that one's got 'em all beat, Eddie replied.

Jet suspected that Eddie was not referring to the horse but Adele.

Later at the stables, Adele had just finished cooling Sangfroid down and was brushing his shiny black coat. She stroked slowly letting thoughts of Jet fill her mind. Things had to change. She had been pinning for Jet for four years now. It was time she did something more than taking advantage of every opportunity to be near him.

The first time she'd laid eyes on Jet, he was standing in their front yard which was an auto salvage yard. Blackie, their Doberman guard dog was growling and barking up a storm. Adele was sitting in the chair swing on the front porch of their mobile home, reading *Gone with the Wind* for the tenth time. A black Jaguar car was driven into the yard. She put her book down to quiet Blackie.

Driven by curiosity, she had gone out to see what the stranger wanted. Once she had the dog under control, the man had cleared his car, thus giving Adele a full glimpse of him for the first time. And what a sight. Adele had realized that the man of her school girl fantasies had become flesh and blood. Even from a distance often feet, his piercing black eyes had mesmerized.

Adele had gawked like an idiot. Obviously amused, he had explained with a knowing smile and wink that he wanted to see her daddy. He had placed a business card into Adele's unsteady hand and told her to have her daddy call that number. Then he had settled that gorgeous frame of his into his fancy car and drove away.

Up until that day, her life had consisted mostly of old movies, music and books. She had been such a bookworm it had made her very unpopular at school. She'd been glad to graduate from high school early, at sixteen. Adele loved to write almost as much as she loved to read. She had put all her longings for success and Jet's love into her writing. Using the pen name Tremaine Randall, she had been quite successful in writing short stories for romance magazines and she already had a publisher for her first full-length historical romance novel.

Only her parents and her agent knew that she was Tremaine Randall. She wasn't about to give the people of St. Pien-e, another reason to slight her. During her senior year of high school, most of the kids had poked fun at her for being a stablegirl. But she had ignored their laughter and continued working in the stables because it gave her ample opportunity to see and be near Jet.

Now that she was in graduate school and working toward becoming a professor of history, it was imperative that it not be known that she was the author of sultry romance novels. If her college professors became privy to that information, she would never be considered a serious scholar of history.

But Adele didn't have the time to consider that particular problem. She had a more urgent problem to solve—Jet. She wanted him to make love to her, desperately. But it wasn't about to happen. Jet wasn't about to let it happen. The man had too many scruples to get involved with his stablegirl. Somehow she would bypass Jet's strong sense of honor and seduce him.

How was she going to make it happen, when she and Jet never were alone together? Jet saw to that. Although Adele was inexperienced, she knew enough about men to know that Jet was attracted to her. Though Adele knew what she had to do, she still didn't have an inkling on how she was going to make it possible for her and Jet to be alone together. How in the world was she ever going to make that happen?

Jet loved watching Adele. At this point in his life, watching her when she wasn't aware of him doing so, gave him more pleasure than anything else on earth. It gave him much more pleasure than the ideal of becoming a billionaire. It amused Jet to no ends that she perceived herself as such an orchestrator, manipulator. Her lovely features were far to expressive, revealing, to allow her to be a true manipulator. Yet, she could be outrageously unpredictable at times. This fasinated Jet.

Today, was a treat, indeed. His little spitfire was plotting something. Her pretty forehead with its widow's peak was creased in deep concentration and her beautiful almond shaped eyes were almost squinted shut. Yes, she was up to something. Something momentous. Instinctually, Jet knew that he was the object of her scheming.

Adele so engrossed in her thoughts was oblivious to how diligently she was working. She'd long since shed Jet's jumper and was bared to a short-sleeved tee-shirt and her overalls. A thin veil of perspiration covered her arms, neck and face causing her deep brown skin to glisten almost as much as the sable coat of the horse whose mane she was slowly but vigorously brushing.

Jet inhaled deeply to slow down the pounding of his heart. Not only was she lovely, she was down right sexy. Even the baggy overalls she was wearing could not hide her curves. She had a body that would have moved Marilyn Monroe to envy.

The spreading weakness in her limbs and the tingling sensations along her spine warned Adele of Jet's presence. She continued her stroking of Sang-froid's mane at a much slower pace.

Jet's warm gaze caused cool slivers of excitement to streak through her causing the tiny beads of perspiration that covered her body to feel like showed off his powerful thighs and sexy rearend. She positively ached for Jet to make love to her.

God, here was something new. She wanted him. Invariably, Jet's passion swelled and surged in him, threatening to break through the dam of control he had carefully constructed over the past four years.

The bold way her eyes raked over him from head to toe almost drove Jet to the point oflosing control. He could barely restrain himself from grabbing Adele and crushing her to him and kissing her senseless.

Jet shook his head to clear it. Hadn't college taught Adele anything about the way of the world? Sweet lord, she was a graduate student. Didn't she know better than to stare at a man the way she was staring at him? Instead of staring back at her like a love starved ranch hound, he had to get out of that stable before he gave her what she obviously wanted from him.

"Look, Adele I appreciate the great job you've done with Sangfroid." He really did drink the wind to his voice trailed off. God, how lame could he get, but he had spoken the first thing he could think of to say, dared say.

"Although he is only half Arabian he is a drinker of the wind, Adele noted, repeating the phrase that Jet had taught her to use to refer to an Arabian horse's running ability. God, he had taught her so much, and she wanted him to teach her the most important lesson of all—making love.

Dammit, she was doing it again, looking at him in that way ? His soul burned for her and was saying the the things he dared not say. *Adele, if I don't make you mine soon, I think I'm going to go mad from wanting you so much.*

God, it was maddening wanting her the way he did and knowing he couldn't act on his feelings. Adele was still too young and she had a lot of growing up to do, moreso than most young women her age.

The smouldering look in Jet's eyes excited and frighten Adele. But when had she ever let a little fear stop her from doing what she wanted to do? The sexual tension between her and Jet had become palpable. Adele felt compelled to speak, to ease the tension. Her heart was still beating a wild rhythm against the back of her throat. And she struggled to drag her eyes off Jet.

"I remember the night Sangfroid was born," she said, turning her attention to the horse whose ears were perked as if he sensed the tension. Adele planted a kiss on the horse's satiny forehead right between the ears.

For a moment, Jet fervently wished he was the horse, the receiver of Adele's kiss.

"It was storming that night," Adele said, nozzling the horse with her nose were she had just kissed him.

"Hurricane going on but you were fearless." Jet reminisced, swallowing the lump in his throat. If anything had happened to Adele that night, his life wouldn't have been worth a plucked nickle. "I wanted to shake you for coming out to the stables on such a night."

"I had to. I had a premonition that Desert Storm was in trouble." "And, you were right." Jet expression turned remorseful. I should never have bred her with such a large thoroughbred.

"You did all that you could to take care of her. You gave her the best veterinary care available. Adele tried to lessened his feelings of guilt.

Jet nodded. It wasn't enough to save her. Damn. Guilt and remorse still tore at his insides. Sangfroid was such a large foal. His size in addition to his breach birth ripped her insides to shreds." On the heels of his words, an uninvited and disturbing question raced to mind. *Is Adele to small to have my babies.* Once more, Jet's eyes roamed freely over Adele's curvaceous but petite body. His silent question made Jet feel both cold and hot at the same time. He blushed, something he hadn't done since he was fifteen.

Adele wondered if the bold way she had been staring at him was the cause of Jet's obvious embarrassment. For a moment she felt contrite, but only for a moment. Jet needed to get over his scruples and get with the program. Hell, he wanted her every bit as much as she wanted him.

Mon Dieu, she's staring at me in that maddening and provocative way again. Sweet lord, he couldn't take much more of it. He had to put some distance between them, immediately. Noticing his jumper on the stall post, he reached for it and started to leave.

Panic rose up in Adele. He was leaving. She couldn't bear for him to leave just yet. "I am afraid that coat smells of horse, now" she stammered slightly. Somehow, she had found her voice.

Her sweet husky voice nailed Jet in mid-stride. He couldn't leave. That's okay, its washable. "I'll just throw it in the washer," he replied, turning and facing her.

An unsurpressable giggle escaped Adele's lips. The image of the rich and powerful Jacques Trideaux doing his own laundry was just too much.

Jet took a step toward Adele and pinned her with a piercing glare.

"So you think my doing laundry is funny," he observed with a playful smirk. "Yep," Adele agreed immediately. "It's hard imagining you doing something as mundane as washing your own clothes," she added with tongue in cheek.

Once more Jet manage to suppress the strong desire to kiss her senseless. "And just how do you imagine me?" he queried boldly. God, he was playing with fire but couldn't seem to help himself *"Naked and on top of me"*. Adele cantered silently. She immediately regretted her wayward thoughts when she felt the rising heat of a blush. Besides, it was obvious that Jet already knew how she imagined him. To her chagrin, she realized that Jet was greatly amused.

A glint of laughter danced in his dark eyes. Adele was incensed. The heat of her rising ire matched her burning embarrassment. Did he think that she was some silly little girl that he could play with and take lightly. Well, she would show him as she had shown all those in St. Pierre who had made fun of her and unestimated her over the years, Adele swore silently. Jet would rue the day he so callously underestimated her.

Though it was a dangerous game, Jet was having the time of his life playing with his little spitfire. "You haven't answered my question. Answer it", he demanded, softly.

He had some nerve, to think that his silly question deserved an answer, Adele fumed silently. Well, hell would freeze over before she gave him one. Instead, she decided she would ask him a question. One that was a little less, unsettling. "Why are you doing your own laundry? I thought you had a live—in lackey. Oh, I mean housekeeper, Miss Aucoin," she added impishly.

"A few days ago, Miss Aucoin rushed back home to Barbados to be with her very ill sister", Jet explained with an ease he didn't feel. He concentrated hard on what he was trying to say and did his damndest to ignore the rise and fall of Adele's breasts beneath the snug fitting tee shirt.

"It seems she going to have to stay and help her sister recuperate," he continued. "So I guess, I have to rough it," Being in close proximity to you is rough, he thought.

The even tone of his voice had masked his disappointment at the tum the conversation had taken. It would make his day, his week, just to see her blush again. He particularly adored the way her blush made her deep brown skin take on a rosy hue from the neck upward. No way, his little spitfire could ever pass the paper bag test. This fact didn't make her any less dear to him.

A light went off in Adele's head. What was it that her mother was always saying? *There's no ill wind that blows all bad,* or something like that. Here was her chance to be alone with Jet. She could become his housekeeper.

"I could do it." "Do what?"

"I could become your housekeeper." Adele crossed her fingers behind her. "At least for a little while, anyway," she added quickly.

Jet knew he was going to say yes, even though his brain screamed. No! The little minx was up to something for sure. And he had an inkling what it was. So why would he risk getting caught in another one of her little schemes, especially such a dangerous one? Because it was time. It was time he started training her, molding her into becoming the kind of woman his lifestyle demanded. Adele's little plot offered him the perfect opportunity to do so.

Jet decided he would have a little fun with her before he gave his answer.

"So, you're interested in becoming my lackey. Oh, I mean housekeeper," he bantered. Why? Jet gave her a probing look. "I would think a brilliant graduate student such as you would have her pick of part-time jobs." He eyed her suspiciously. And what about your class schedule?"

Adele squirmed a little but she wasn't about to let him best her. I've been offered a couple of jobs, but they don't pay as well as you do." As for my class schedule, I'm on spring break right now and in two of my classes I turned in my assignments early and have finished the work for the semester. The other two are all on Tuesday and Thursday afternoons. Adele explained in a single breath.

She wondered how she had been able to talk so fast, considering the way her heart was pounding in her throat.

"Jet chuckled warmly. Somewhere in all that you said, you did admit that I pay well. He gave an exaggerated sigh. Believe me, its a relief to know that you do give me credit for paying my lackeys—my help— well," he teased. His voice vibrated with merriment. "Sometimes, I think you see me as a Robber Baron of sorts."

"I don't see you that way at all," Adele acknowledged softly. She stiffened her back and force herself to look him in the eye once more. The gentle smile in his eyes made her heart stand still. Adele could feel her ire, her temporary refuge, slipping further away.

"Well, how do you see me?' Jet drawled. "You know you did not answer me the first time I asked." He could have pinched himself with glee at the 360 degree turn of the conversation.

"And I have no intention of wasting time answering a question in which you already know the answer," Adele admitted, derision back in her tone. She fought desperately against the urge to throw herself against Jet and beg him to kiss her until she fainted or something. Instead, she ignored the agonizing ache that rent her, and sparred tenaciously. "And you didn't answer my question—one that truly warrants an answer." Do I have the job, or not?"

Jet couldn't decide if she was better when she was embarrassed or when she was holding her own with him. 'The jobs yours, if that is what you want." He shot her a penetrating look. I still don't understand why you would want to spend your spring break cooking meals and cleaning my home. And besides, are you willing to give up all this?" He motioned to the stables.

"I like to cook." Adele explained sincerely. And I can always come down and visit Sang-froid."

Jet almost bought it. But he knew better. She had already cooked up something for him. He couldn't resist the urge to tease her a little bit more. Remembering the jacket, he held it to his nose and inhaled. "Adele, you're wrong about the jacket, your sweet scent has overwhelmed the smell of horse, as you've overwhelmed me," he drawled flirtatiously. Hoping to make her blush once more, Jet gave Adele what he hoped was his hottest wink and chuckled softly when it got the desired results.

Adele's anger was hotter than her face. She hated it when Jet made her blush. She invariably felt immature and unsophisticated. How on earth was she ever going to seduce him if she continued to blush like a country bumpkin whenever his eyes fell on her?

CHAPTER TWO

Jet was on his way out of the stables and still chuckling to himself when Eddie stopped him at the entrance.

"Mr. Trideaux, I was in the stables a few moments ago and I couldn't help overhearing." "Do you think it wise to hire that young gal as your housekeeper, feeling the way you do about 'er"

"You don't miss a thing do you, Mr. Thibodeaux?"

"Nothing 'escapes these old eyes. "And besides", he laughed outright.

'I would have to be blind not see how you feel about that one.". "It shows that bad, does it?"

"I reckon it do, to those who really know you." Man, I've watched you for the past three years or so, let that Iii gal wrap you around her little finger." Now, you've gone and let her talk you into letting her run your house." Why you go and do a lame thing like that?" Hell, you know what's bound to happen when that girl moves into your home."

"Oh, no.' Jet laughed. I'm smarter than that. "She's only going to work days, parttime at most." "I'm going to see that she is safely deposited on her parents doorsteps each evening."

"Un huh, you better." Cause the gossipmongers would have a field day, ifthey ever caught wind of you having a young gal living with ya."

"Don't worry, Mr. Thiboudeaux, I've got it all under control." Jet said, as he strolled off in his usual confident swagger.

Eddie Thiboudeaux, sighed deeply and shook his head. He was convinced that trouble lay ahead for Jacques Trideaux. Adele Baychan was a scandal waiting to happen. But maybe he could do something to defuse the situation. What that girl needed was a good old-fashion eye opening. And he had just the thing that might make that lil gal see the light.

Adele was pitching hay into an empty stall when Eddie Thibodueaux approached her.

"Take a look at that." He thrusted a magazine at her.

Curious, she dropped the pitchfork and took the book. Her breath caught in her throat. On the cover ofthe business magazine was a glossy close up picture of Jet. Decked out in a dark business suit he was more handsome than she had imagined he would be on the cover of a magazine. She began to ache from the top of her head to the bottom of her feet.

Though her hands were shaking like leaves on a tree in a summer squall, she managed to find the article. The title ofthe article "Prince of the Creoles", screamed out at her.

Adele forgot that Eddie was watching her as she flipped the pages in rapid succession 'as she speed read about Jet's business acumen and latest business deal in which he had closed a 200 million dollar deal in New Orleans for a gambling casino.

According to the article, it was the largest business buy out ever made by an African American. Albeit, the author used a lot of print to describe the Trideaux family history. Jet's pure Creole blood-lines could be traced back 200 years or more.

There was a picture of Jet at his French Quarter mansion with his socialite mother, Mignon Eldemonde Trideaux. Also, there was a picture of Jet at some big ball with a Virginia business woman and socialite, Paulette Joseph. She could also trace her pure Creole blood lines back about 200 years. The writer hinted that they would probably announce their engagement in the near future. Adele's heart sanlc She didn't have much time. If she was going to seduce Jet, she would have to do it soon.

Agitation covered the young gal's features. She seemed almost sad. Eddie felt remorse. He hadn't expected that reaction. He'd expected the girl to show pride, even cockiness that such a man as Jacques Trideaux was so smitten with her.

He just wanted the girl to realize that she needed to start acting more ladylike and stop putting Mr. Trideaux in sticky situations. The future Mrs. Jacques Trideaux had no business pitching hay in a damn horse stable. Because one thing he knew as sure as the sun would rise the next morning, when Jacques Trideaux married it would be to his Iii stablegal. "Now you listen to me good, young lady, I know Mr. Trideaux is a very down to earth sort around here, but that doesn't make him any less famous or important." And don't you forget it."

"Mr. Thiboudeaux, I couldn't forget that, even ifI tried."

"Well, you need to start acting it." What Mr. Trideaux needs is a real ladylike sort."

Adele closed her eyes for a second against the bum of her unshed tears. "Something I could never be."

"I bet you could be, if you tried."

"I know that I can't be one ofthe beautiful people like Jet and Paulette. I use to dream of being popular. But the few times I tried to fit in I failed miserably."

"I find that hard to believe," Mr. Thiboudeaux scoffed." You such a pretty Iii' gal."

"It' takes more than prettiness to be one of the beautiful people." "Adele tried to push back the evading memory of once overhearing one of her teachers refer to her as "the beautiful misfit." Sheilding herself with the armor of her pride, Adele said, "I don't want to change. It took me too long to learn to like and accept myself as am and I'm not going to try and reinvent myself into becoming something I don't care to be anymore, not for anyone."

"Not even for Mr. Trideaux?"

"Not even for him. Besides, what would be the point?"

"Mr. Trideaux is real sweet on you." He just might ask you to marry 'em.

"I doubt that." People like Jacques Trideaux don't marry their stablegirls."

"Mr. Jacques not like that. Not a stuckup bone in his whole body." "That's might be so, but I'm no thoroughbred debutante either." Eddie threw his head back and laughed outright. "You don't say." "I don't think he's looking to marry up with a horse."

Adele laughed, then said, "Maybe not. but he will probably apply the same principles that he uses in breeding thoroughbreds in choosing the future mother of his children."

"You sho' have some misguided notions about Mr. Trideaux.

"I realize that you've known Jet for a very long time. Still, I think I have a pretty good inkling of what makes the man tick."

"Young lady, what you know is the Jet that everybody sees today, I knew him when he was just plain Jacques, Jr. "You know, his Mama and friends started calling him Jet because of his initials but some folk started calling him that because of how fast he can tum a dollar into a million dollars. "Faster than the speed of sound, they say." He chuckled. But that's another story. He scratched his head and squinted. "Let me see. I started working for the Trideauxs at their place out in Chalmette when he was small. I set him on his first horse and taught him how to ride." He beamed. That young man always loved horses. "So, I reckon I know him about as well as anybody."

"Mr. Thibodeaux, what was Jet like when he was a young boy?" It was hard for Adele to fathom Jet as a young boy or even a teenager.

Mr. Thibodeaux look away for a moment before he answered.

He was like any other young man, I suppose. "Having a good time, getting into mischef. But when his father died in a plane crash when he was about fifteen, it seems he grew up overnight. Became serious. I reckon, he figured he had to fill his daddy shoes."

Adele's heart ached for the young Jet who had to grow up too soon. There was little wonder that his jet black hair was dashed with strains of gray. He would gray prematurely.

Eddie Thiboudeaux knowing eyes, recognized genuine concern for Jet in Adele's expressive eyes." The lil gal really did love Jet and not his money. He was as sure of that as he was sure that she was the one that Jacques Trideaux would marry. If ony she would learn how to be the kind of woman Jet needed. Otherwise, she was going to add to not ease the pressures of Jet's life. Maybe she would wise up after looking in that magazme.

Mr. Thiboudeaux, left the magazine with Adele and got busy about the stables. He just hope that he had finally put that girl on the right road to becoming the kind of wife Mr. Trideaux would need.

That night at home, Adele mauled over the article. Each time she looked at the picture of Jet with Paulette Joseph, her heart was clutched by talons of pain. Time was running out for her, somehow she had to make Jet make love to her before he became engaged. Once he became engaged, he would become totally and irrevocably forbidden. The next day she would start her job as Jet's housekeeper, despite her parents misgivings.

Adele was determined. She would experience lovemaking for the first time with Jet. He was every girl's fantasy. She bet he would be a terrific lover, though he wasn't good husband material, at least not for her. Though she enjoyed reading and writing fairytales, she knew real life didn't work that way. Ironically, her success at weaving fairytales had made her face the reality of the situation. If she and Jet were to marry their lives together would be a nightmare. It wouldn't be long before Jet would grow impatient with her for saying the wrong things, doing the wrong things, or most likely, wearing the wrong things.

Yes, she would have her one night oflove with Jet and put it behind her. It would put an end to the silly crush she had on him then she could move on with her life. she would start dating and eventually she would probably find and marry someone more compatible—a college professor, perhaps. The wife of a college professor didn't have to worry about saying life. Yes, her Professor X and she would have a good life together, one filled with books, music and academia.

Albeit, she couldn't began to seriously comtemplate such a future until she got Jet out of her system. The the best way was to have one night with him then move on. Somehow she would make that happen. A short while later, she drifted off to sleep chanting softly, "I must make it happen.

I will make it happen." Afterall, she had the perfect plan.

CHAPTER THREE

"Dam it!' Adele swore as the glass shattered about her feet in several large pieces on the marble floor. She grabbed a nearby broom and frantically tried to clean up the dangerous mess. All the while she bemoaned herself for being such a careless klutz. It was only her fifth day as Jet's housekeeper and she was proving to be incompetent. How in the world was she going to tell Jet about the flower vase. Though it was made of plain crystal glass, it had screamed old money. It was obviously an antique. She'd just put a fresh bouquet of gardenias in it when it had slipped from her fingers. She had wanted to impress Jet with a fresh bunch of flowers from his yard. Getting accustomed to working in Jets house had been difficult. She hadn't anticipated the intimidating affect that the opulence of the house would have on her. All week long, she had been ill at ease.

'Fiveforks" Jet's house was the most spectacular house in the area. Built in the neoclassical style, the mansion was situationed on a hill that overlooked a bend in Fiveforks River. Many times, Adele had marvelled at the exterior of the house but the interior was even more impressive. It was finished in white marble, solid brasses and dark mahogany wood throughout. The house actually had its own ballroom that was the entire south wing. Jet's mansion only reinforced what Adele already knew. Jet was eons out of her reach. And she probably had as much chance as a lame horse winning the Kentucky Derby of getting Jet to make love to her. ranted out loud. When she was upset, she sometimes talked to herself. "You're not, and I would never fire you."

The unexpected sound of Jet's voice behind her caused Adele to jump and she cut her finger on the large piece of glass she was holding. It wasn't a very deep cut, yet, in an instant crimson spots stained the shiny white marble floor of the breakfast nook. Jet was at her side in an instant. He rushed her to the sink and held her finger under cold water.

"Danm my carelessness." Jet swore angrily."!shouldn't have startled you like that when you were dealing with broken glass.

Adele looked on miserably, as Jet gingerly wrapped her finger in a dish towel. Nothing was going as planned. Instead of serving, perhaps even sharing, a cozy little lunch with Jet, she was bleeding all over him and the feminine but sexy little flora dress she was wearing.

After applying direct pressure to the cut for a moment, Jet unwrapped the towel to see if the bleeding had slowed. Once more, blood squirted from the cut like a geyser. Acute concerned clouded Jet features.

Adele felt like giving herself a hard kick for creating such a mess. And she resolved to put an end to it. "Jet it not as bad as it seems. I bleed freely, that's all.

Jet was still unconvinced.

Damn, she would just have to show him, she was okay. "My platelets are slow to coagulate. "I'll be okay if you let me get to the sugar bowl.

Moments later, Adele generously applied sugar to the cut.

To the amazement of Jet, in seconds, the geyser was dormant. "So that's why you always look so sweet." Jet teased.

Not to be outdone, Adele flirted back. "I taste even sweeter." She gave Jet a coquettish little smile.

Jet's heart did a somersault at the mere thought of kissing Adele. Things could get out of hand in a New York minute if he wasn't careful.

"Putting all kidding aside, Adele are you really going to be okay, now?" Jet gave Adele a solemn look.

"Jet you're such a worrywart. Really, it's nothing. It looks worse than it is. Adele tried to reassure Jet, once more. However her hurried words, did nothing to smooth the worry crease in his forehead. He took her by the shoulder and guided her to the small eating area off the kitchen, and seated her gently at the table.

"I want to make sure you get some food into you as soon as possible so that your body can start to regenerate the blood you've just lost."

"Really, Jet I'm going to be fine. "It's your beautiful vase that's not okay. "I'm so sorry." Adele ended with a soft sob.

"Don't give it another thought." I can buy another vase to replace that one. "But you are irreplaceable, Adele." His voice trembled slightly. He couldn't bear to see her cry.

Adele notice that his large hand still rested about her shoulder even though she was seated. The little blood she had left rushed to her head. She was heady.

Noticing the wild little pulse beat in her slender throat, Jet had to fight back the urge to cover it with his lips then slowly kiss his way to its source, her heart. God, how he ached for her. Seeing her in his home like that looking so vulnerable and beautiful was almost to much for him to endure. He was on fire.

The heat of his hand poured through the thin fabric of the dress and melted into Adele's shoulder and seem to premeate its heat throughout her body, her soul. She raised her eyes to look upward into his eyes. There was no mistaking the glitter of passion's fire in their ebony depths. He wanted her. And she wanted him too. The magnolia blossoms ofthe cheery wallpapering of the breakfast nook faded from her vision as she became consumed by a red haze of desire. Her almond shaped eyes slanted almost shut as she continued to gaze into Jet's eyes. She wanted him to make love to her so bad. She felt as if she was going to die. Her heart was racing madly. Her lips parted invitingly and begged silently to be kissed.

Mon Dieu. The little vixen was driving him beyond control. He sensed in her a passion that was akin to his own. Somehow he would have to find the strength not to succumb to what was happening between Adele and him. They were alone in the house he had built for her and it would take all his resolve to behave honorably. His basic instinct was to sweep her up into his arms and carry her up the winding staircase to his bed. He inhaled deeply and counted to ten silently.

"Something smells delicious." He blurted out suddenly. "Let me see what delights you have whipped up for me today. He was already headed for the kitchen.

A sharp knife of disappointment cut Adele to the quick. How could he tum off his feelings like that? Apparently he didn't desire her as much as she had thought.

"Stay where you are. He called back to her. I'll bring the food out." An amazed Adele, looked on as Jet proceeded to do the task that she should've been doing. In a matter of moments, he had efficiently set the meal of grilled trout, garden fi·esh nibblet com and a tossed salad and French bread toast on the table.

"I can't believe you prepared such a scrupulous looking feast from the list of bland foods my diet allows." He beamed. He took a seat opposite Adele at the large round mahogany dinette.

"I hope you find the meal as tasty as it looks. I tried to do a good job. Adele watched anxiously as Jet forked a bite of the grilled fish into his mouth. He savored its taste for a long moment before he swallowed. "Urn, Mon ami, c'est ce bon!"

Adele, sighed at the double-edged compliment. Jet's cute little French phrase had let her know that she had been successful in cooking a delicious meal that would not harm his ulcer as well as dash her hopes of ever seducing him. He saw her as a friend. Was that all she would ever be to him, a friend? No. She wanted more, much more. And she was going to make it happen.

Adele took tiny little bites of her food, as she watched Jet devour his meal with haste. The midday sun beamed through the pristine white lace curtains that draped the large bay window. It provided an excellent background for Jet's tall frame. The bright glare of the sun exposed the profound attractiveness of the man. Up until that moment, Adele had not had time to really take stock of what he was wearing. Now, she took note. He was dressed in a dark brown plaid suit that had almost obscure black stripes. Instead of a dress shirt and tie, he had chosen a black silk crewneck shirt. Of course, the shirt bore the signature monogram of Jet in brown embroidery. The man was a perfectionist. How could an inexperience country girl such as she ever hope to seduce such a worldly man. But somehow, someway, she was going to make it happen. Afterall, she had managed to make it possible for Jet and her to spend some time alone.

"Penny for your thoughts my petite amour." Jet's warm drawl dragged Adele from her reverie. She was disconcerted. "They're not worth even that. She snorted. One moment, the man called her a friend and in the next moment, he was showering her with sweet endearments.

Jet suppressed a smile. It was wrong to tease her so. But it was such joy to watch the play of emotions on her lovely features. Besides the little vixen deserved it for all of her schemes and finagles. Jet didn't bother to conceal his scrutiny. He stared at her boldly until she began to chaff. And he received his objective. He felt something akin to bliss as he watched the blush travel from the swell of her breast that rose provocatively above the low neckline of the little dress to her face. It was a great effort for him to keep his breathing normal. Little doubt, she was wearing a push up bra.

Mon Dieu. She didn't need any help in that department at all. But it was all part of one her little plot to seduce him. He would wager his business empire that she hadn't left home that morning in that dress. No way,

Zechariah Baychan and Lorraine Baychan would have let their only child leave the house with her breast spilling over the top of her dress that way. Most likely, she had put it on when she had gotten to his house. Yes, the little vixen deserved his teasing. And he was about to give her a dose of her own medicine. He had a few schemes up his sleeve too.

"After your accident today, I don't think it would be prudent for you to go with me to the races tomorrow." You need to take it easy for a few days." He studied her briefly, then forked the last of the meal into his mouth.

"I'm fine." Adele almost shrieked. "We're talking about a cut finger, Jet. That's all. You've talking as ifI've severed a limb or something." She pouted. She wouldn't be able to bear it if she didn't get to see Sang-froid in his first horse race. Surely, Jet realized this.

"Well, you did bleed a lot. Are you sure you're up to it?"

"I'm positive." Adele responded immediately. She was too upset to give import to the little smile that played on Jet's lips. Take a look. She thrusted the cut finger across the table toward him.

"Urn, huh." Jet demurred.

"Now, that I've got my hopes up about going, There is no way on God's green earth I'm going to miss that horse race. I'm going if I have to walk all the way to New Orleans." Adele threatened.

If the stubborn set of her chin was any indication, she would. Jet knew. Enjoying his little game immensely, he continued to appear unconvinced. He rubbed his chin thoughtfully as he continued to study Adele. "Well, before you start your long march to New Orleans, I want you to march up those stairs to my bedroom and get those bunch of boxes that are under my bed." He commanded playfully.

"I'm in the library." Jet called to Adele as she stepped off the last step of the staircase.

When Adele entered the library he was perched on the edge of the large mahogany reading desk. He long legs were crossed at the ankles.

Adele walked over and placed the packages beside him on the desk. She stood back and grasped her hands togather. Waiting.

"Aren't you going to open them?" Jet queried softly.

Adele was baffled. She didn't know what to make of the brightly colored boxes. "What's in them?"

"Open them and find out." Jet urged. Then he eased off the desk and casually strolled to a large leather winged chair and sat down. He crossed his legs and sat waiting.

For once, Adele was at a total lost for words as she removed a dress and its matching coat of the most beautiful and softest fabric she had ever touched. She stepped back and held it against herself.

"It just a little something I picked up for you at Harrods in London." Jet told her. There was a catch in his voice. Her awed reaction left no doubt that she like what he had chosen.

The two piece suit consisted of a silk shantung halter dress in a hot fuchsia and its matching blazer. There were other boxes to open which she did so eagerly. In one box there was a flora wicker handbag. And in another box there was a fuchsia bow hat that had a square crown with a wide soft mesh brim. Also, there were fuchsia leather sandals with one and one-half inch heels. Jet hadn't forgotten a thing. One box contained some jewelry. The pair of small earrings and bracelet were made of delicate pink pearls. There was even a large Gucci makeup bag full of expensive makeup that was perfect for her coloring.

Adele didn't know what to make of it. One moment Jet was ruthlessly teasing her and in the next instant, she discovers he had done something so nice for her. "Why did you buy me all these lovely things?" I had planned on wearing a pair of my favorite jeans." She had to stifle a giggle at the grimace that covered Jet's face.

Therein is your answer baby." Adele heart skipped a beat at his light use of the sweet endearment.

"We are going to be the winners tomorrow." That I am sure of. And I want to make sure we look the part. There was a strange light in his dark eyes that Adele couldn't fathom.

Adele had never seen Jet like this before. What was really going on with him?" She wondered. But she wasn't going to let his odd behavior concern her now. She 'ld think about that later. Right now, she had clothes to try on, makeup to experiment with. She was so excited she could burst. But before she began, she would have to thank Jet properly. Where was her manners? Adele quailed her excitement momentarily.

"Thank you," she told him and gave him a coy smile.

Adele's shy little smile went to Jet's head. He spoke without thinking. "You're quite welcome. This is just the beginning."

"What do you mean by that?"

"I mean to buy you lots of pretty things from now on." Don't you like pretty things?"

"Yes, I do but that's beside the point." I don't think that it would be appropriate for you to shower me with gifts." "Why not?

"You know."

Warming to the game, Jet grinned. "No, I don't." That dress for instance would you call that appropriate attire for the workplace? Yet, you're wearing it. So why shouldn't I buy you pretty things?

He was deliberately baiting her. Adele fought for control of her temper. "Do I have to spell it out for you?"

"Please do."

"That would make me a kept woman."

Jet laughed. "Not so. In order for you to be my kept woman, we would have to be lovers." I have no intention of letting that happen."

Adele planted her hands on her hips. "Why not?"

Jet studied her for a long moment then he bestowed on her one of his indulgent smiles that he knew she hated. "Because you are an infant." He teased.

That was to much for Adele to endure. "Jet, I will have you know that I am an extremely accomplished woman of twenty whose capable of taking care of herself. With the money that I make from writing I can buy myself pretty things. I don't need you to buy me gifts as ifl am some pet you intend to spoil.

"You are my pet. And I intend to spoil you outrageously." He winked. He uncrossed his legs. "As always I find it hard to pull myself away from your charming presence but I really need to head back to the office." He heaved himself from his chair and swaggered to the door. In the broad doorway, he paused suddenly. He turned to face Adele.

"Adele, ifi ever find you in such a dress at work again, I'm going to pick you up, throw you over my shoulder and pack you back to your parents to change."

Adele sputtered. "You wouldn't?"

"I certainly would and you know it." He gave her a rogue's wink and swaggered out.

Adele fought the urge to grab a large volume fi·om a floor to ceiling bookshelf and throw it after him. Most of all she wondered if her perfect plan of seduction was doomed tofailure.

CHAPTER FOUR

The two story office building that Jet had built near his cellulose plant was made of gray stone and had a green metal roof. It should have looked foreign amidst the pine and oak tree forest in which it set. It didn't. To the contrary, some how its traditional French townhouse design and striking beauty seemed to enhance its surrounding. Because of its existence the green straws of the pine trees seemed greener, and the oaks seemed taller, more majestic. Jet had designed the office complex himself. He wanted to be sure that his office building as well as the plant be environmentally friendly.

Even the products produced—toothpaste and soaps— were organic. They were produced from the cellulose—the chief part of the cell wall of plants. The plants were harvested from the surrounding forest or grown in the soybean fields ofFiveforks. Jet had a comer office that had floor to ceiling French window doors that opened unto a veranda. Magnolia plants, wild ferns and pieces of deadwood that had been taken from the surrounding forest were used as palt of the office decor. He had an excellent view of the beautiful forest from a large comer window. Often he would stand in front of the window and watch the squirrels and an occasional deer family. Staring out in the forest usually helped him to get a handle on things whenever he was troubled. This day was such a day. Long after he was back in his office, Jet continued to stare out into the forest. Of course, he was thinking about Adele. It seemed that he couldn't think of much else recently. 'Was he making his move to soon? Was Adele ready for what lay ahead? She had never been anywhere with him away from the ranch. One thing was for certain, in view of recent developments in their relationship, it was just a matter of time anyway. But was this the right way and the right time to introduce Adele to his world.

"Come in please." Jet responded to the knock on his office door. Zechariah Baychan stared for the moment at the back of the man who was still staring out the window into the forest. Then in an uneasy surge his blue eyes washed over the large fancy office.

"Have a seat, Mr. Baychan. Jet said, as he turned to face the man he had summoned to his office. Jet's dark eyes almost did a double take. Even to this day he still was amazed by the metamorphis that had taken place with the man. The clean cut very fair-skinned man who was seating himself, bore little resemblance to the man he met three years earlier. The first time he had met Zechariah Baychan, his skin had been darkened by over exposure to the sun and his old jeans and shirt had been covered in old oil and dirt. Now dressed in a starched and ironed Jet Enterprises uniform, the man looked very much the competent maintenance supervisor he had proven to be. The only thing about the man that looked exactly the same was the ocean blue color of his eyes. Even his hair was different. Hair that had appeared to be brown and curly was actually blonde and without a hint of a curl. The only resemblance to her father that Adele possessed was the auburn highlights in her long dark hair. Adele's darker skin coloring had came from her mother, Lorraine Baychan, who was as dark as the rich soil of the delta.

Eyes as blue and fierce as the North Atlantic Ocean locked on Jet as he took a seat on the opposite side of his desk.

"Mr. Baychan, I'll get right to the point. Jet began. "The reason, I asked you to my office today is that . . . Jet's voice faltered. The man was glaring at Jet as if Jet had just stolen something from him. "It's about Adele." Jet began once more.

But before Jet could say another word, Zechariah Baylor stopped him. "I figured as much. "It's about that trip to New Orleans, that Adele has been raving about." "Well, Mr. Trideaux, I'm glad you called me in today, because if you hadn't I was coming in to see ya' myself." His eyes flashed angrily. "I'll get right to the point." I don't like the idea of you buying Adele all those fancy clothes. "She was raised to be a decent girl, and she can't be bought, Mr. Trideaux.

"That's goes without saying." I know that Adele . . .

"Did ya know that she fancies herself to be in love with you?" "Yes, sir, I do. And I . . .

"For these past few years, I watched my little girl hang around you like a little love starved pup. I been hoping she get over this silly school girl ctush of hers.

Zechariah Baylor, had no inkling of the anquish his words caused Jet.

Was that all Adele felt for him, a silly school girl crush that would fade with time?

"Well, she has her heart set on going to this horse race. And I ain't never been able to refused that girl anything that was in my capability.

"So, I am asking you as a father, and I want you to promise me, Mr. Trideaux. You will not take advantage of my little girl. I want you to promise me, you gonna bring her back in the same condition you took, her. Pride and anger glittered in his blue eyes like streaks of lightening on the ocean's horizon.

Fire and ice. Jet thoughts wandered for a second. The heated glare in Zechariah Baychan's eyes brought that thought to mind.

"Being a man, I think ya know what, I mean." Zechariah drove home his point.

Jet did. "I give you my word, Mr. Baychan."

Jet was fond of Mr. Baychan, and he respected him. Usually their conversations were quite amicable. Zachariah Baychan had proven to be a great asset to Jet Enterprises. Jet was glad he had taken a chance on him inspite of the advise of others who had told him the man lacked the self-discipline for the job. The man could fix anything. He kept the machinery at the plant humming. Furthermore, the man was computer literate. Jet wanted to stay on solid footing with the man, hopefully,' he would be his father-in-law one day.

"Mr. Baychan, how's the website going?

It's going great, I've been getting orders pretty regularly. That was a great idea you gave me. Since I've been listing my rare classic auto parts on the internet, I've made over a hundred thousand in sales."

"That's great, Mr. Baychan." And I bet it gets better."

Zechariah studied Jet from a moment. His earlier gruffiness had lessen somewhat. "Mr. Trideaux, you brought a lot of prosperity to this area, and my family. And like most people in this area, I'm beholding to ya'. But what I want you to understand, Adele is my daughter, the only child I've got. She's precious to me. "And I sure won't be beholding to ya' if you take advantage of my Iii girl."

Jet, eyes didn't falter as he met Zechariah Baychan's fire and ice glare head on. "I promise you, Mr. Baychan, I will not take advantage of Adele."

Jet's driver picked Adele up at eight as Jet had promised when he[d called the night before. He'd told her to get a good nights rest and be ready to go at eight the next morning. Adele had been so excited. But out of a desire to look her best the next day, she had willed herself to fall asleep. She had actually managed to get a full eight hours rest. When she made up her mind to do something, she did it.

"Where are we going? She asked the driver. "Aren't we going to the stables to pick up Sang-froid?

"Miss Adele, Sang-froid is already at the stables near the race track down in New Orleans. He was taken there late yesterday afternoon. So that he wouldn't be skittish for the race. Anthony his rider is down there with 'em too. And we are going up to the airport to meet up with Mr. Trideaux.

Adele was confused. Why in the world did they need to go to the airport? She had a sudden sense of foreboding.

The moment they arrived at the airport, Jet rushed up to the car and helped Adele get out. He took her by the elbow, and started steering her in the direction of his small passenger plane.

Adele stopped suddenly, in mid-stride. "I don't understand. "Surely, you don't expect me to get in that thing?

"Yes, I do. C'mon baby. We don't have much time. He coaxed.

But Adele wasn't bulging. She had never flown before and she wasn't about to fly for the first time in something so small.

"C'mon, Adele. "You can do this."

II "No, I can't. She shook her head adamantly.

Sounding a bit exasperated, Jet reminded her. "This can't be the same gutsy Adele who threaten to walk all the way to New Orleans because she wanted to see her horse race for the first time."

"At least, my feet would be safely on the ground." Adele shoot back. Jet had some nerve to insinuate that she was behaving cowardly. She hated showing this weakness but she couldn't help it. As she looked about the paved plain of the airfield, she thought. *Everything is so easy for Jet.*

She wanted to go so bad. And she would go, even if she had to go in that damnable airplane. Adele fought back her terror and began to inch toward the waiting plane.

She was trembling as Jet strapped her into the passenger seat immediately behind the cockpit. The plane, a Piper Mirage, seated six, therefore, it wasn't as small as Adele had first thought. Her trembling lessen a bit, but not much.

Concerned over her obvious distress, Jet cupped her chin and gently forced her to look at him. "You trust me don't you Adele?"

Adele nodded.

"Then, you know I would never let anything bad happen to you. "I'm going to be flying the plane. He gave Adele's chin a playful little pinch. "I promise I'm going to take good care of you.

At Jet's gentle reassurance, Adele fears began to subside.

Once they were airborne, Adele admitted to Jet that it wasn't as bad as she had anticipated. Jet's easy banter and invariable teasing soon caused her to relax. Jet was happy as a lark to be flying. He loved flying but didn't get to do it often enough he admitted to Adele.

Jet flew in low over Lake Ponchartrain so that Adele could have a good view. She knew he was showing off to impress her with his expert handling of the powerful plane. It gave her a warm feeling inside to know that he thought her important enough to impress. The sight of the sunlight bouncing off the tranquil blue waters of the lake below almost took her breath away. She was actually flying in a plane. *Unbelievable.* She thought.

"That's the Causeway down there" Adele exclaimed. As they made their descent, Jet followed the path of the world's longest bridge over water.

A few minutes later, they landed at Lakefront Airport at the mouth of Lake Ponchartrain. Once they were on the ground, they hurried across the pavement to a waiting stretch limousine. By now, Adele was enormously impressed by Jet's style and savvy. During the plane trip, Adele had resolved not to be intimidated by Jet's wealth. She was going to enjoy her day with Jet to the fullest. It was not until they were in the limo that she notice what Jet was wearing. He had on a Jet black suit, pristine white shirt, and black suspenders. The unique part of the outfit was the specially designed tie. It was Jet black. There was a hand painted picture of a horse and jockey in its center. The jockey's cap and jacket were fuschia.

Adele recognized the artistic trademark of a New Orleans designer, Jean Claude, that Jet patronized quite often.

"Adele, forgive me for not saying it before now, mon petite amour, you are a vision ofloveliness in that outfit." "Isn't she, Mother?"

Adele had been so wrapped up in Jet and a bit giddy from her first flying experience she hadn't notice that they were not alone in the huge car. "Mother you remember Adele Baychan. "Adele, my mother, Mignon Trideaux."

"How do you do, Mam." Adele managed a squeak. She wanted to crawl into the rich black leather upholstery of the limo. She sounded so gauche. She felt especially so when Mignon Trideaux surmised her to be of no import with a cultivated chuckled and wave of her well-manicured fingers. "Of course I remember her. You pointed her out to me when I visited your stables during the Christmas holidays. Good gracious, she's your little stablegirl."

Over the wide brim of Adele's hat, Jet shoot his mother a warning glare. Not that it would do any good, he knew. A pang of worry for Adele caused his stomach to tighten. Was she ready for his mother and her set? Mon Dieu, would she ever be ready for that bunch of elitists? He loved his mother dearly, but he wasn't under any delusions about her short comings.

Mignon Trideaux spent the next five minutes of so, totally ignoring Adele and talking to Jet about people and events that Adele hadn't the slightest inkling of. Adele's pride rose in her like a foal standing for the first time—weak and wobbly.

She decided she would pretend that Mignon Trideaux's snobbery wasn't affecting her in the least. She did her best to concentrate on the Old World charm of the Vieux Carre' as the limo crawled through its narrow streets. It wasn't long before her love of history dominated her thoughts. New Orleans was one of Americas oldest cities. It was over 270 years old. Furthermore, it had such a rich blend of Old World and New World culture and heritage. As they passed the Cabildo, Adele's discomfort forgotten for the moment, remarked to Jet. "Do you know that in 1803 from November 30th to December 20th the flags of three nations flew over it—Spain, France then America," she elaborated then fell silent.

"Mother, in case you haven't already surmised from Adele's significant knowledge of history, Adele is a scholar of history. "She;s working on a Masters in History at the University of Southern Louisiana."

"Oh." Mignon Trideaux demurred.

Adele's eyes followed the elder Trideauxs eyes as they fell to the Harvard ring worn by her son." Adele imagined she could read the lady's thoughts. *Good gracious, a state university is afar cry from Harvard.* Ordinarily, Adele would have laughed off Mignon Trideaux's obvious snobbery. She couldn't. For some unfathomable reason, Jet's mother's obvious disapproval hurt. Albeit, Jet was by her side. Adele drew strength from that reality. She wasn't about to let Mignon Trideaux spoil the precious time she had to share with Jet.

"I can't believe it." Adele blurted out. "Can't believe what?" Jet queried calmly.

"That's the House ofRhythm."

"What of it? To Adele's amazement, Jet gave a nonchalant shrug. "What of it?" She mimicked Jet. "It's only the coolest, hottest nightspot in New Orleans, maybe the entire delta."

To say that she was perturbed by her son's obvious infatuation with his little stablegirl would have been an immense under statement. Mignon Trideaux was cooly livid. Her gloved hands tightly clutched the straps of her eel skin purse as she watched the lively verbal exchange take place between her son and the little gold digger. Jet looked so at ease and comfortable with this girl. *Good gracious, could her son actually be considering marrying the little upstart. Heaven forbid! She had to make sure that didn't occur.*

"The House of Rhythm is all that, uh? The slang phrase slipped easily from Jet lips. Not to be outdone, Adele cantered. "All that, and more." She laughed.

The musical quality of her laugh caused Jet's heart to swell with love to the point he thought it would burst. It was such sweet torture to be near her.

"Tell me more, about this place." His serene demeanor denied his inner turmoil.

Adele began to list off a bevy of popular rhythm and blues artists and groups who had and would be performing at the infamous nightspot.

"Jet gave his mother, who knew that he was the owner of the club, a roguish wink.

"Adele, I'm surprised you know of the existence of those muscians, even moreso, that you actually listen to their music.

"Not only do I listen to their music, I dance to it, also." She told a baffled Jet.

"But, you weren't even born when most of that music and the dances were popular."

"I know. But I happen to think that the rhythm and blues music of the 60s, 70s and 80s was some of the most beautiful music ever written."
"Well, that sure makes you different then the rest of your generation". But, you're not like anyone I have ever known.

This is serious. Mignon Trideaux thought.

Outside the limousine, the bright sunlight made Mignon Trideaux's perfection more obvious to Adele. For the age of sixty or any age, Mignon Trideaux was a strikingly beautiful woman. Her makeup, hair and nails were flawless. Her outfit, a two-piece column dress with a white and black embroidered top and a classic black skirt, and the accentuating black bow hat, screamed class. Adele knew that she looked comparably good in the outfit that Jet had bought for her. Albeit, she knew that Mignon Trideaux looked that stunning every day of her life. Adele had a sinking feeling that Jet's wife would also have to live up to those standards. She could never pull that off. She loved her overalls and old worn hats too much not that it mattered. Jet would never consider marrying someone such as she, anyway.

CHAPTER FIVE

It was just a little past midday and the day had turned out to be a surprisingly sultry one for early April. Adele wondered if it would be worth the effort to touch up the small amount of make up she had applied that morning. She quickly quailed the notion. A glance at Jet, told her he was his usual unruffled stolid. The only effect the intimidating heat had on him was to cause a thin little mist of perspiration to form on his forehead. His pristine white shirt looked as crisp as when they had first started out. *How does he do that?'* She wondered.

"Now, aren't you glad that you're wearing that silly ol' hat, I bought you." Jet teased Adele as they took their seat in the stands of one of the owners boxes. "Adele pinched Jet on the arm for throwing up her words to her. She really felt like pinching herself, to test whether or not she was dreaming it all. "It's me Sang-froid beneath the fancy duds and silly ol' hat" she had told the horse who seemed a bit anxious when she had approached him in the stables. "You know, I never meant for you to hear what I said. "Do you always sneak up on people like that?"

"No. I only sneak up on cute little enchantresses to find out what they really think about what I've bought them."

"I love the outfit that you bought me." Adele exclaimed fervently. "It's just that I don't like hats."

"Yes you do!" Liar! "Jet chided playfully. He tried to look very stem which was impossible. There was too much laughter in his eyes.

"Well, I do like hats, Adele admitted sheepishly. It's just that, well I don't like this kind of hat. She pointed at the maligned hat on her head, and rolled her eyes upward. "It's just not me."

"I guess, it will take me some time to figure out what you like." He told her. *"But that's okay because I plan on spending the rest of my life trying my best to please you.* "He thought. He decided it was time to change the conversation. It was best to finish their conversation at another time. A time when he and Adele were not in the presence of his very observant mother.

Jet reached inside of his pocket.

"What's this?" A bewildered Adele looked down at the handful of crisp new hundred dollar bills Jet had just taken from his money clip and placed in her hand.

"It's for you to make a bet." Don't you want to bet on Sangfroid?" Jet gave her quick directions where to go and she was off to place her bet. Then he eased his long frame, once again, into a bleacher seat next to his mother. He was ready to be the buffer between his mother and Adele, if the need arose. Most likely, it would.

The moment Adele was out of hearing distance, Jet turned to his mother. "Mama", I don't like the way you've been looking down your nose at Adele."

"I have done no such thing." She protested weakly.

"Yes you have." And stop it. I mean it Mama. "Stop it." "I want you to promise me, you're are going to make an effort to be nice to Adele." "I care a great deal about her.

The situation was serious. That was the second time her self-reliant son had called her Mama in a matter of seconds. He reserved the endearment of Mama, for those rare occasions when he really needed her acqmesce.

"I can see that you are smitten, son." "But she's very young, Jet. "What are you trying to do, regain your lost youth or something?" Ignoring her son's scowl, she continued. "Besides, you have nothing in common with this young woman."

"I love her, and if she loves me, what else do we need to have in common Mama?"

"Social class and heritage, for a start." She retorted. She fanned herself with her handkerchief all the while her eyes darted about the stands as if she was surreptitiously looking for someone.

Noticing her odd behavior, Jet deigned not to comment on her last remark. Instead he demanded. "Mother is there something or someone special your eyes are raking the stands in search of?"

Mignon Trideaux, hesitated for a moment then decided that her best bet was to be straight out with it. "Paulette's in town on business. When we talked last night, she said she might drop by to lend you support on such an important day.

"Mon Dieu." Jet mumbled under his breath. He gave his mother a look of utter disbelief. The last thing he needed was for Paulette Joseph to show up, now. That would only make an already delicate situation all the more difficult.

"Twenty to one, little lady, that's the odds." The bored ticket salesman told Adele when she placed her bet. "Is that for or against Sangfroid?'

"Against, Mam." He drummed his hands on the counter. "Are 'ya going to place a bet or not?"

Adele laid the ten one hundred dollar bills on the counter. 'Sangfroid in the seventh race to win.

"You sure you don't want to bet Win, Place or Show, Mam?" I hate to see a pretty little gal like yourselflose all her money."

"I'm sure." And I won't lose my money."

The man's air of boredom dissipated. He studied the beautiful girl in the fucshia outfit, for a moment. "What do you know about that horse that's makes you so sure, he's gonna win?"

She gave him a tiny little smile that didn't reach her eyes. Then in a tone so soft the man had to lean toward her in order to hear, she told him. "I know his bloodlines. It's all about bloodlines. It is the bloodlines that separate the winners from the losers.' She took the proffered ticket and started back to Jet and his mother.

Yes, Sangfroid had the right heritage. His sires blood could be traced back to the founding studs that produced such great throughbreds such as Man of War and Secretariat. His mother Desert Storm had been a pureblood Arabian.

Unlike Sangfroid, she lacked bloodlines. She didn't have the heritage or background that would win her a permanent place in Jet's life. That withstanding, it was urgent that she have her moment of passion with Jet before it was too late. She felt she was running out oftime.

When she arrived back, to her dismay, there was a beautiful woman sitting between Jet and his mother. She recognized Paulette Joseph immediately. Her first instinct was to hightail it out of there and run and not stop running until she was back in St. Pierre. But on the heels of that notion was a great surge of prideful anger. Even the beautiful and accompolished Paulette would not be allowed to spoil her moment in the sun with Jet. With as much grace as she could muster, Adele took the seat next to Jet that he had saved for her. After the protocols had been taken care of, Adele gave Paulette the once over from head to toe. It seemed it was a day for bow hats. Paulette had on a sophisticated little black and white bow hat. The rest of her ensemble consisted of a black and white polka dot silk dress and a matching white blazer. Paulette defintely could live up to Mignon Trideaux's standard of dress. But she wasn't going to let the Paulette Josephs of the world concern her right then. Her main concern at that moment was the horse she had loved from the moment of his breach birth, her baby, Sangfroid. And he was just a baby, in horseracing age he was considered a three year old but in reality he was just barely two and one half years of age. Sangfroid was being positioned into the seventh shoot. That was too near the end. Poor Sangfroid would have to start his first professional run almost on the outside. This wasn't good.

"Adele turned to Jet." "Jet aren't you concerned about Sangfroids starting position?" She queried anxiously.

"Not in the least". He gave her hand a reassuring squeeze. This tiny action however didn't go unnoticed by the other two women. They gave each other a conspiratory look.

"In fact, I am very pleased with his position." Jet gave her one of his cocky little smiles.

Adele's heart skipped a beat.

"His position makes him the number seven horse in the seventh race of the day. Jet elaborated. The number seven has always been good to me."

Still Adele was not convinced that all would go as expected. "Jet, I am afraid the people who laid the odds don't support your confidence." Have you seen the odds."

"I have."

"Didn't you report Sangfroids bloodlines." "Had to." Was his dispassionate reply.

His nonchalance was beginning to irk, Adele. For a moment, but only for the briefest of moments, she wondered why she loved Jacques Entione Trideaux so very much. They were so disparate. She was easily excitable and he was usually cool as a cucumber.

"Then why such odds against, Sangfroid." Adele wondered out loud. "Babe, its his first race. And Sangfroid didn't train locally. There's the chance he might be intimidated by it all. Jet explained patiently.

"I doubt that Sangfroid would ever be intimidated by anything or anyone.'1 Adele was thore than a little miffed that anyone could doubt the superiority of her baby. Don't those ninnies know that the name Sangfroid means cool. She pouted prettily.

Jet threw his head back and laughed. He loved it when she did that.

It was as nature to her as breathing. She didn't even know that she did it. "I don't think everyone is as up on their epistemology as you Adele, he laughed.

Looking on, Mignon Trideaux, wondered if she had ever heard her son laugh so much. *Indeed, the situation is dire.*

"And they're off!" At the sound of the announcement, the butterflies in Adele's stomach went mad. Sangfroid made a bold start, showing that he was born to it. He was in third place when he reached the first tum. But as Adele had suspected because he was on the outside he had to tum wide. Adele's heart sank as he fell to dead last She couldn't watch her baby not do well. But like a moth is drawn to the flame of a candle, she was compelled to watch the infamy. She was sqeezing Jet's hand so hard, she had to be hurting him. She ignored the smarting of her cut finger.

"Come, on boy, you can do it". Jet chanted softly." Move him to the inside Anthony, he urged the jockey with a bit more force.

Anthony leaned forward on Sangfroid as if he was talking to him. The dynamic will of Jet must have been sensed by the horse and his jockey, or maybe it was the desire of the horse to win. Adele couldn't believe what was unfolding before her very eyes. Sangfroid was moving to the inside and passing up the other horses. Watching him do that, made it difficult to believe that before that moment he had only raced against practice gallopers. By the time he reached the second bend he was third in the row, and in third place once more. When he took the final bend he was second, then first as he came into the home stretch. Adele was on her feet screaming at this point,. so was Jet. She didn't know if she had pulled him up with her or vlce versa. There was a great roar in Adele ears. She didn't know if was the noise of the horses hooves and their heavy breathing or it was her blood pounding in her ears. At that point in the race the horses were so close to the stands she wondered if Sangfroid could hear her screaming to him. "Come on my beautiful black baby. "Show 'em your stuff!"

Then Sangfroid simply walked away from the rest of the horses leaving them far in his wake as he flew across the finish line.

"Unbelievable!" Went the annoucer.

What happened next was as unbelievable as the race. Adele found herself being lifted off her feet by Jet and swung about in his arms. For a brief moment, his lips were on hers. The brief little kiss superceded everything else for Adele. The cheering crowd in the stands, even Sangfroid fell into the background of her thoughts. *Jet just kissed me for the first time.* That thought was paramount.

"Yes, Jet yelled. He sat an unsturdy Adele back on her feet. *And to think I deemed this man, dispassionate a few minutes ago.* Adele couldn't resist touching her lips for a second, lips Jet had just kissed.

What happened was pure mayhem. Some of the other owners were congradulating Jet and his mother. Paulette Joseph gushed. "Jet is there anything that you can't do." "Jet you did it." You said you would and you did." His mother cried proudly. But through it all, Jet kept a firm hold around Adele's waist.

Adele thought she was in a fairytale dream that she didn't want to wake up from. She was actually being positioned to take a picture along with Jet, Anthony, and Sangfroid in the winners circle. The newspaper, and televisions camera were flashing and rolling. It was about to go out on national wire that Sangfroid had broken the track record. He had won the race in two minutes and thirty seconds, just one second behind a recent Kentucky Derby winner. Louisville, Kentucky would most likely be the next race for Sangfroid.

When Adele had gone to collect her winnings. Mignon Trideaux was able to get close to her son.

"Jet, I'm apalled at the outrageous spectacle of public display of affection that you and your little stable girl made here today. Most of the major black magazines are represented here today—Jet, Ebony, the whole lot. You forget everything that you do makes the headlines these days. She gave Jet one of those *I am very displeased* looks that he hadn't received since he was a little boy and had gotten into mischief. Do you have any idea how many cameras went off when you kissed that girl in broad daylight in this public arena!"

"No, I don't Mother." "And I could care less" Besides, they are here for biographical information today, that picture will not make the magazines unless I win the Derby. He explained half-heartedly. All Jet really wanted to think about was the memory of how it had felt to hold Adele in his arms for those few moments. Nothing else had ever felt so good and right. "Excuse me, Mother. I have business to take care of." Jet walked away, leaving his mother to stare after him, her beautiful features determined.

"*Now where did Paulette get off too? She had to find Paulette so that she could initiate her plan of damage control.*

CHAPTER SIX

Adele looked at the twenty-thousand dollars in her hands. She had never held so much money in her hands before. She had received a twenty five thousand dollar scholarship to college. But it had not been paid directly to her. Each semester a portion of it was paid directly toward her college tuition and books. The twenty-five-thousand dollar royalties advance that she had received from Notions book publishers had gone directly into her account under the name of Tremaine Randall. But she would think about what she would do with the money later. All she really wanted to think about was Jet's kiss. It had lasted only a second or two but it had rocked her world and left her pinning for more, much more. That kiss promised so much.

While Jet and Adele was preparing Sangfroid for the trip back to Five forks, Mignon Trideaux and Paulette Joseph went on ahead to Jets house. After giving Sangfroid a heroes send-off back to Fiveforks, Jet told Adele that they would be having a little celebration party at his home on St. Charles Avenue in the Quarters.

"You've got to get something new to wear Jet told Adele as the limo eased through the busy downtown area of the city. "You've been in those bright colored duds all day. I think you need something just a little more sedate for my party this evening."

"Jet, why did you choose fuschia as the color to represent Fiveforks." Adele wondered out loud."

Jet paused a long moment before he answered. There was a strange light in his eyes. "Once upon a time," he began. "I drove into this salvage yard and this vision, what I thought was a vision at the time, a beautiful girl dressed in a fuschia colored old-fashioned style gown, came out to greet me. As she held her vicious guard dog in check, the wind blew her black mane of riotous curls in the wind." Adele if live to be a hundred, I will never forget the first time that I saw you." His words though beautiful and romantic, stirred feelings of unease in Adele. Was Jet teasing her?" *God, could he possibly know about the steamy historical romance I have written. I will just die, if he does.*

When Jet had first began his little tale about the day they met, Adele's body as if of its own volition had moved closer to him. Now that she suspected that he had only been teasing her, because somehow, someway he had found out about her book, she wanted to put some distance between them. She was tempted to move away from Jet, but something about the way he was looking at her nailed her to the spot.

No. Jet wasn't about to let Adele get away that easy. Ever since he had read the excerpts from the book she had written, he had been tom between the urge to take her over his knee and spank her and the urge of throwing all caution to the wind and making love to her the way she had described it in her lovemaking scene. At that moment, the latter urge had the upper hand. Mon Dieu, what was he going to do about this girl-woman who set his body and soul on fire.

Adele knew he was going to kiss her even before he took off her hat. She had known by the burning look in his eyes. Then he lowered his head ever so slowly. It seemed like a million years, for Adele was impatient to feel his lips again. Finally, his lips claimed hers ever so gently. And with tender little strokes as light as the brush of a feather his tongue and lips began to make love to her lips. Their mouths were the only part of their bodies that were touching. Jet continued to kiss her in that tortuous fashion for what seemed like an eternity. His lips played a sweet melody, a love song on her lips. Adele wanted to deepen the kiss, but when she tried to put her arms around Jet, he stayed her hands forcing them to stay pressed against the car seat. And he continued the gentle ravishment of her mouth. The maddening kiss was both heaven and hell, ecstasy and agony. Desperate to deepen the kiss, Adele wantonly parted her lips beneath his. Jet pulled away abruptly as if she had touched a lit match to his mouth.

"We're there." Jet managed to get out. He sounded short of breath as if he had just ran a race himself. Adele hadn't even noticed until then that the limo had stopped moving. They were in front of an elite boutique on St. Charles Avenue.

"Aren't you going in with me?" Adele asked anxiously.

"No, kiddo, I'm afraid I have to stop off for a while at my corporate office down the street. "You're be okay. "You're got a purse full of money. You can buy whatever you want."

Adele had forgotten about the money, she had won. "What if i buy the wrong thing?" Adele queried anxiously.

"You're do just fine. Jet asssured her. "I trust your judgment, baby." And he did. It was his judgment that he was beginning to questioned. What had processed him to kiss Adele? He had almost lost complete control.

The little minx's sudden and total surrender of her mouth to him had almost been his undoing. As the limo pulled away from the curb, Jet poured himself a drink of scotch from the bar. He knocked it back in one gulp. He didn't give a fig at that moment what it would do to his ulcerated stomach. Wine was too sweet. He needed the fiery drink to eradicate the maddening sweet nectar of Adele from his mouth. Otherwise, it would be just to damn difficult for him to concentrate once he was at his office. With a wenching pain in his gut he could concentrate, but he could not form a coherent thought with the incredibly sweet taste of Adele in his mouth.

Le Boutique Orleans was like no other boutique in which Adele had shopped. It was possible to purchase a complete outfit from the shoes upward. Jet had said that she needed something more sedate. What could be more sedate than black. Adele chose the classic little black dress in a crepe silk. She chose three and a half inch black pumps in the same matching material. The tall heels would make her stand almost five feet eight inches. Which was a more compatible height to Jet's six feet—two inches. Then she chose sexy black undetwear and the sheeriest, most satiny black stockings imaginable. To relieve the black a bit, she chose a string of expensive faux pearls and the matching single pearl earrings. She told one clerk that she needed to get dress there in the store because she was going to a party at Jacques Trideauxs in a short while. Shortly afterward, all the clerks were bending over backward to be helpful. Adele was taken to a plush private dressing room in which to dress by no less than the store manager. One of the clerks even helped Adele restyle her hair. In order to wear the hat, Adele had brushed her thick hair into a tight pony tail in which she had braided. The helpful clerk parted Adele's hair in the center and combed her hair to one side and sort of twisted it into one large loose braid that she draped to the front. She also helped Adele apply her makeup, skillfully. The earthy orange lipstick that the clerk chose for Adele really accentuated the black outfit. She told Adele that particular shade would drew attention to Adele's beautiful brown eyes, as well. When it was all done, Adele took a look at herself in a full-length mirror. It was well worth the five-thousand dollars she had just forked out. She had accomplished her goal. The outfit made her look classy as well as sexy. She gave an impish little smile at her reflection as she preened. Yes. She was dressed. Dressed to seduce.

Adele was sitting primly on a Louis XIV loveseat in the entrance foyer when Jet walked into the boutique. There was a flurry of excitment. But none of that mattered to Adele as she stood. Her main concern was the man whose eyes were telling her that she looked beautiful.

"Well done. Well done, Madamoiselle" Jet beamed. He crooked his arm and Adele took it.

Jet's house was a sprawling antebellum three-story that had been built around 1820. It had an unusually large front yard for New Orleans. There were wrap-around verandas. It had been built by a rich banker, Leland Trideaux, who was rumored to be one of Jet's white kinfolk. Leland Trideaux had loved to entertain. Therefore the house had a rich history of balls and high society antebellum galas. During the Civil War it had been used to quarter Union soldiers during Butler's occupation of New Orleans.

When Jet and Adele arrived, there were already a long line of cars parked out front and the long driveway at the side of the house was lined with bumper to bumper cars. Adeles heart was fluttering and her stomach was quivering with butterflies as she alighted from the limo. She was so nervous. Though the flagstone walkway was well-lighted by colonial style lamps, Adele missed a step.

"It's going to be fine, Adele."

Adele felt panicky. "Jet, I don't know any of those high-fuluting people that are in there." "I probably won't know what to say or do."

"You know me. And you do just fine with me. I always thought I was high-fuluting?" He laughed. He made a funny face that made Adele laugh as well.

In front of the massive stained plate glass door, Jet took a deep breath and let it out slowly in the manner of man who has arrived at a decision and knows that there is no turning back. Then he opened the door and entered with Adele on his arm.

The moment they walked in, a heavy silence fell over the large living room. But Adele hardly noticed. It was the house that was recipient of most of her attention.

Unlike Fiveforks, this house did not intimidate Adele. Fiveforks, represented wealth. This house exuded history. Every board, every chrystal chandelier was authenic. Of course, she was awed by its grandeur. But for the most part, she loved it for all the history that had taken place there.

"Look at how the little golddigger is sizing up the house. "Can't you just see the dollar signs in her eyes?" Mignon Trideaux whispered loudly to Paulette Joseph. Both women had been watching the door for Jet and his little companion.

"My, my, she is so obvious." You would think Jet would be able to see through her. Paulette observed maliciously.

"Huh!" Men what do they notice." They can't get past a pretty face and a hot little body." "I'm afraid my son suffers from the same affliction as his brethen." "That's why Paulette, it is imperative that you and I put our heads together so that we can save Jet from himsel£"

Paulette nodded in agreement. Then the two women entwined their little fingers and shook on it.

Jet introduced her to the twenty or more people present, who ranged from the Mayor and his wife to a former U.S. ambassador.

"Jet how did your mother get all these important people to come to your party on such short notice. Adele asked at first chance.

"Jet laughed before he answered." Most called to congratulate me, most likely and my mother invited them to our little celebration."

Adele parceled him a look of incredulity. "What you're saying is that when Jacques Trideaux beckons even former U.S. ambassadors come running."

"Jet chuckled. Amusement gleamed in his eyes. "No. I'm not saying that. You asked me a question and I answered it sincerely." "Besides the former ambassador is my second cousin." He's family.

Adele didn't know what to make of it all. Why did Jet invite her to his party? She was confused. But that was Jet. She never knew what he was thinking, yet, he always seemed to know exactly what she was about." It really irked her.

"Don't you want to see the house? Or would you just rather stand around and fi·own at my guests?

"I'm not frowning. Adele argued.

"Yes you are." Jet took Adele by the armed and started giving her a brief tour of the downstairs part of the house. Adele loved it all. The dark wallnut panel walls, the double staircases, the glossy stained wood floors.

Jet was showing Adele the dinning room when his mother and Paulette Joseph joined them.

"I see Jet has been showing you around, Adele." "What, you think?" Mignon Trideaux, gave Adele a tight little smile that was more of a smirk than anything."

"Yeah, tell us what you think?" Paulette piped in. The two women gave each other a knowing look.

Adele knew that they didn't mean her well. They had an ulterior motive for seeking her opinion about the house. She studied the two sophisticated women with their Cheshire smiles. Something was afoot. God, why was she putting herself through all of this drama? She wondered for the upteenth time since she had entered the party. *Jet.* That's why. She would do anything, go anywhere just to be with him. Since she had chosen that path, she just might as well accept the consequences that came with the territory.

"I love it. Adele answered sincerely." As Jet told you, Mrs. Trideaux, I'm a history major. The lover of history in me could not help but love this house." Adele could see immediately, that the two ladies hadn't expected that answer and were not hiding their disappointment very well.

The tension between the ladies became a palable thing. Jet felt that he had to do something before he found himself in the mist of an old-fashioned cat fight.

"This house since it came into our family in the early 1900s has seen a lot of history which has been chronicled in the photos that cover these walls. He made a sweeping motion with his hands toward the picture heavy walls.

There were pictures of Jet's grandparents having dinner, on separate occasions, with W.E.B. Dubois, George Washington Carver, and Carter G. Woodson. There was a photo of Jet's father and mother having dinner with Robert F. Kennedy and in another they dined with Dr. Martin Luther King, Jr.

"My mother was carrying me at the time, and that dinner occurred about a year before Dr. King was assasinated in Memphis." Jet explained to a very overwhelmed Adele.

"I can't believe all those famous people actually set at this very table and had dinner." Adele cautiously touched the lace table cloth of the large table that was the center of the dinner room and the center of Jet's family history. Upon closer inspection of the pictures, Adele noticed something that she hadn't notice at first because she had been focused on the distinquished personages in the pictures. Her eyes burned with unshed tears.

In each picture in the center of the table, filled with roses, was the vase—the vase she had broken at Fiveforks.

"You gone awful quiet all of a sudden." I finally found something that could make you be quiet." Jet teased. Then the laughter in his eyes died when he saw that Adele was starring at the vase she had broken.

Jet notice that Adele's obvious distress hadn't gone unnoticed by his mother and Paulette. Knowing how his mother felt about Adele already, the last thing he needed to do was to explain that Adele had broken an important family heirloom.

"Let's blow this joint." Jet whispered in Adele's ear.

"But it's a celebration party for you." Adele protested weakly. God, she really did want to get out of there. Mignon Trideaux's scrutiny burned into her back.

"I've spoken to everyone. "I've even had a glass or two of champagne."

"Don't you want anything to eat?"

"No." Strangely, he wasn't hungry. He was full of the joy of just being with Adele.

Jet, told his strongly protesting mom, that he and Adele were leaving. "But Jet, if you leave now that will show a lack of social grace on your part." His mother told him.

Jet wasn't daunted. He shot his mother one of his most charming smiles. "Mother I trust you to carry on in your very gracious and capable manner.

"But, what will I tell our guests?"

"Tell them I was called away on urgent business". "It has happened quite often in the past." Besides most of them won't even notice that I'm gone. He nodded toward the champaigne fountain that his guest were freely helping themselves to. He laughed then kissed his mother on the cheek. "Jet this is very childish of you." His mother fumed.

"Yes it is." Jet agreed wholeheartedly.

Jet steered Adele toward the front door. They reached it without anyone really taking note. Then they were on the veranda. They both gave a sigh of relief and giggled. Like two children they ran hand in hand down the walk-way to the waiting limosine.

Chapter Seven

"Are you hungry?" Jet asked Adele as the limosine pulled away from the curb.

Adele shook her head. God, who needed to eat. She was too excited to think about food. Besides, the only thing she was hungry for at that moment was the taste of Jet's kisses. She wanted more than anything in the world to kiss him at that moment. The memory of how Jet had seemed more concerned about her than the vase when she had broken it kept running across her mind. Jet was such a kind and good man. It was little wonder that she had such a crush on him. With all the nerve she could muster. Adele eased closer to Jet and planted an unsure little kiss on his cheek. "Thanks." She told him.

"For what?"

"For being you."

She is so sweet and innocent. Jet thought. It was very diffficult for him to behave himself when she looked at him with those beautiful eyes aglow with love. Mon Dieu. He needed a drink. This time he wisely chose chilled white wine from the bar.

"Aren't you going to offer me any?" Adele pouted prettily. "I'm old enough to drink."

"No you are not." "The legal drinking age in this state is still twenty-one. Besides, you haven't eaten anything. "It's not good to drink on an empty stomach. Maybe he should follow his own advice, he mentally chided himself. But could he really expect prudence of himself when he had allowed himself to fall hopelessly in love with a woman who was younger than the legal drinking age? He took a big gulp of the wine and emptied the glass which he immediately refilled.

Adele stared at the sweating glass of wine longingly.

"I ate a few finger sandwiches and some French pastries at Le Boutique Orleans." Adele prevaricated.

Relenting, Jet let her take a sip fi·om his glass. She giggled as she turned the glass to make sure she drank from the exact spot Jet had drank. She took a greedy swallow. When she attempted to take another gulp, Jet took the wine from her causing a tiny little bit to spill on her lower lip and chin. He couldn't resist the urge to lick the wine off. Adele's mouth opened to the kiss like a morning glory opens to the sun. Jet groaned and dropped the empty wine glass. He enfolded Adele in his anns and captured Adele's tongue with his.

Adele gave a soft little whimper of pleasure and gave herself totally to the sweetness and splendor of Jet's kiss. She wanted to get even closer to Jet, but when she tried to pull him closer, her atms seemed boneless. And this weakness was spreading. She felt like she was going to die, go crazy. She didn't know. All she knew was that she didn't want Jet to ever stop kissing her. The more Jet kissed her, the more she wanted. She began to kiss Jet back in the manner he was kissing her. She nibbled at his lips and she captured his tongue with hers.

He surrendered to her for a moment. Then he did the unthifl_kable. He stopped. He gently pushed her away.

Adele felt bereft. How could he kiss her into a senseless bundle of jelly then just stop like that? How could he? Adele watched in disbelief as he calmly straightened his clothes took out a handkerchief an. A dull knife of jealously cut through her. Jet was worldly. 1 here were probably lots of women in his life. What she needed to do was stop being such a provincial and pretend to be as unaffected as he seemed to be.

"Where are we going?" Adele asked serenely, as she toucht:J up lu::r makeup.

Adele's veneer of imperturbability caused a tiny smile of amusement to play on Jet's mouth. "You'll see. We'll be there shortly." "Aren't you going to tell me where we are going?" "No." He was deliberately noncommittant.

Adele was growing impatience with Jet. Why was Jet being mysterious. Adele wondered. She just hoped that she was dressed okay. For his party,

Jet had dressed down to charcoal grey pleated trousers, the matching jacket and a black silk crew neck shirt. He was elegant casual. "Am Idressed appropriate for where we are going?" Adele asked crossly. She looked down at the little black dress she was wearing.

As if he had read her thoughts, Jet assured her. "What you are wearing will work fine."

Moments later, the limo crawled to a stop in front of the House of Rhythm. Adele let go of a very unladylike sqlJeal of pleasure. But Jet didn't seem to mind.

"I am without a doubt going to show you a very good time, tonight." He bragged as he hauled a very excited Adele from the car.

The moment they entered the large nightclub it became very apparent to Adele that Jet was well-known in the establishment. They were taken immediately to a special table that was reserved at all times for him. Every few minutes a waiter or waitress would drop by and ask if they needed anything. A few moments after they had been seated, the manager came by the table to talk with Jet for a short while.

Once again a dull knife of maddening jealousy cut through Adele. *Jet must bring women here all the time.* She agonized. On a more sane note, she thought. *What has that got to do with you. Jet's not yours and he never will be.* Albeit, she noted." Jet, considering all the solicitous attention we are getting, you must bring your dates here every time you go out on the town.

Jet studied Adele for a moment. He was reading her like a book. She was jealous. He found this very pleasing. Maybe he should let her stew for awhile. But he thought better of it. And answered sincerely. "I've been here lots of times, true. But you are the first woman I've broughl here.

Adele's heart danced with joy.

Watching Adele radiate with joy. Jet could help but think:. *Baby, don't you know. You're a lot of firsts with me.* Besides, it was neither the time nor the place. time and that was what he was going to do.

But it was too soon.

Now that she knew that she was the only woman Jet had brought to the House of Rhythm, Adele was able to notice her surroundings. The club was huge. There was a large dinning area, large viewing screens that showed the performers who were perfmming on the stage in the adjacent area. Then there was the bar.

It had to be the largest bar ever built. It had countless bar stools and about ten bartenders. Those who wanted to sit at the bar and drink could also enjoy the performers on large viewing screens that were strategically positioned behind the bar. The thing that Adele like best about the place was the large dancing area near the stage.

On this particular Friday night a good local rhythm and blues band was performing all the greatest R&B hits from the late 60s, 70s and 80s. Beneath the table Adele's feet tapped to the music. She was itching to dance.

As if reading her mind, Jet asked. "Want to dance?" "I thought you would never ask?" Adele laughed.

In an instant Jet was helping her from her seat and steering her toward the dance floor. When they got onto the dance floor the band was perfonning a Wilson Pickett hit, Mustang Sally and everyone was doing a line dance called the Electric Slide. Adele had done this dance countless times at home in her living room or at weddings. It was easy for her to fall right into step with the other dancers. But it almost put her into cardiac arrest to see Jet fall in step so easily. Not only could Jet do the dance, he was actually very good. Adele soon found herself laughing and giggling as she tried to emulate a cool little step that he did when he dipped and turned. As the band continued to play a lot of Adele's favorite dancing music.

Adele found herself doing dances and steps she had learned from watching old videos and that she had only done alone or fantisized about. She particularly loved the way Jet would swirl her about and then pull her up against him. Jet was a wonderful dancer and so much fun. It was all better than any fantasy could ever be.

Jet could not remember ever feeling so carefree or having as much fun. Watching Adele dance was blowing his mind, and his sense of caution where she was concerned. Adele hadn't notice when her sophisticated little plait had loosen on one of the dance turns. Now, her thick long dark hair flowed about her face and shouders. She glowed from her exertions and joy. Jet was intoxicated, inebriated by his love for her. And his heart swelled with pride too. Adele had caught the attention of just about every male in the club. Who could blame them. It was obvious, that somehow this beautiful woman and the music had become one.

After they did the Hustle, the band fell into a Latin number. Adele was mesmerized by Jet's suave Latin moves. After dancing to a very fast Latin number, Jet suggested they rest for awhile. Instead of going back to their table Jet steered Adele to a bar stool. He ordered two daiquiris, a very low alcohol content pina colada for Adele and a more potent green concoction called a hurricane for himself. Adele's drink was cold and fruity. It was just what she needed, after all that dancing. Adele was enjoying her much deserved drink, and hardly noticed when Jet stopped a passing waiter and told him something.

After they had finished their drinks. Jet asked. "Are you ready to go, or do you want to dance some more?"

"Dance of course."

"That's what I hoped you would say."

This time when Jet and Adele went onto the dance floor, the band was performing a slow number. Adele's heart fluttered like a butterflies wings when she felt Jet's arms go about her and they started moving to the slow beat. When she felt Jet's heart thunder against hers, she decided that she liked this kind of dancing best of all. The music had an earthy slow drag beat. As Adele moved and swayed to its pulsating ryhthm against Jet, she became very much aware that she was wearing only the sheeriest of underwear beneath the little black dress. As she moved against Jet, the sinews of his body caused the heavier material of the dress to caress Adele's body through the sheer bra and panties. Her nipples became hard and turgid.

Jet having long disgarded his jacket, could feel everything through the silk shirt he was wearing. He found himself fighting a storm of desire caused by the sensations of Adele's aroused **little** body being pressed against his. Mon Dieu, he had not thought it possible for him to want a woman as much. For most of his life, his passion had been increasing the family fortune.

After what seemed an eternity, the band ended the song. Jet put a little distance between Adele and himself. The reprieve was short lived.

The lead crooner of the band stepped up to the mike and annouced. "Before I began my song, I want to announce that this song was requested by no other than the clubs owner, Jet Trideaux. This song is dedicated to his sweet young lady in the little black dress."

Adele felt faint. The lights were dimmed even more, and a spotlight found them. She felt like she was caught up in some fairytale that she didn't ever want to end.

Jet had no choice but to dance with Adele. Afterall, he had requested the song. As the singer began his rendition of Freddie Jackson's *You're are My Lady,* Jet took Adeles hands in his and began to sway to the music.

Adele followed Jet's lead. Their hands were the only part of their bodies that touched as they swayed in time to the seductive song. Through their tightly clasped hands, Adele's heart's thunder matched every beat of Jet's heart. The dance was such tantalizing torture. Adele wished that they would pull that damnable spotlight off ofthem so that Jet would take her in his arms once more. As if by magic, the spotlight became history and other dancers started dancing along side them. But Jet didn't pull her close. Adele couldn't bare the sweet torture of being close, yet, not close enough. She literally took matters into her own hands. She did a quick very unladylike little tum that caused her to fall back against Jet. Jet had no choice but to put his arms about her as she did a seductive grind against him. Adele knew her behavior was wicked. But she didn't care. She couldn't help the way that she felt about Jet. She wanted him to make love to her before that night was over.

Jet wanted to take Adele over his knee and spank her perfect little bottom for what she was doing to him on that dance floor. But that delicious image evoked what he had been struggling to avoid most of the evening.

Although her wanton behavior denied her inexperienced, Adele had never felt an aroused manhood before. She felt weak in the knees as Jet's opened palm pressed against her stomach caused her hips to undulate against his pelvic and forced her to feel the evidence of his desire.

"It's too late for you to go all weak and swoon on me." Jet hissed in her ear. "You are going to have to deal with the consequences of your outrageous behavior, my little seductress."

As soon as the song ended. Adele found herself being steered off the dark dance floor. She didn't have time to wonder about where Jet was leading her. She found herself being guided through a door off from the bar that led to a flight of stairs.

Jet's lips claimed Adele's as he slipped a card key in the door and gained entry into the office. When she melted against him, he became besides himself with desire. Not wanting to part from her for a moment, he continued the kiss as he manuevered her farther into the room. His mind searched frantically for a place to love her. The desk was his only choice. He freed one of his hands to clear the desk in a brutal stroke.

Adele was faintly aware of the noise of objects hitting the floor. The sound of her blood pounding in her ears was much louder. Jet was kissing her. No, he was devouring her lips, her tongue. The sweet savageness of his kisses were almost unbearable. Soft little cries of pleasure rose in her throat and escaped into his mouth. Jet's hoarse moan answered her cries.

He unzipped her dress and it fell in a puddle about her feet. Then, he lifted her onto the desk and undid her bra. All the while, he was still kissing Adele. His lips left Adeles and explored a trail to her breast. First he kissed, devoured one then the other. Adele whimpered softly as he suckled one turgid nipple, than the other. Jet's lips left Adele's breast and began to navigate downward. The mist of maddening passion cleared for a moment. This was not the way she had envisioned her and Jet making love. Never would she have imagined that when they made love it would be on top of a desk in some office above a nightclub of people. But as his lips and tongue explored lower and lower, she was caught up in the mist once more. She didn't care. All that mattered was that it was Jet's mouth and hands that were causing the tremors of pleasure that caused her body to shake and qmver so.

The way her delectable body withered beneath him and her sweet little cries of pleasure made Jet want to know her as he had known no other. Jet's mouth navigated pass the top of her garter belt to the sheer little silk panties that she wore. He was enchanted, beguiled when he discovererd that they were tear away. Adele had dressed to be undressed by him. He tore the skimpy little undies off with his teeth. Then his mouth and tongue began to hungrily explore the object of his quest.

His questing lips and tongue evoked raw little cries of pleasure from Adele. Her fingers were entwined in his hair and she kept pulling his head closer causing him to make the most intimate of kisses even more intimate. When his probing tongue sought entrance, it met an obstruction—the evidence of her inexperience.

"I want you to promise me that you gonna bring my daughter back in the same condition that ya took her." Zechariah Baychan's demand came back to haunt Jet. He had promised that he would. And he would not break his promise to Adele's father, even if it just about killed him. Jet rolled off of Adele as if some invisible force had suddenly snatched him away.

"Jet, please don't stop." Adele cried.

Jet raked his hands through his hair angrily, as he looked down on Adele's almost complete nudity. A wave of self-contempt washed over him. How could he have allowed himself to get totally out of control and treat Adele that shabbily.

"Get dressed!" he ordered, his voice was full of derision. He stalked into the restroom. He went to the sank and began to dash his face with cold water. Still the maddening sweet taste and smell of Adele tantalized his senses. He thought about the many cold showers he had taken of late and stuck his entire head under the cold water. He hoped that the frigid spray would as usual numb his desire for Adele.

While Jet was in the bathroom, Adele hurriedly dressed. Suddenly, she was embarrassed by her nudity.

When she had set out to seduce Jet, she had never considered that if she was successful Jet would lose all respect for her.

On the drive back to St. Pierre. Jet and Adele set like two statues. They were emerged in their own world of regret.

The plane ride, Sang-froid's historic win, and all that dancing and what had occurred between Jet and her proved to be too much. Adele fell asleep.

She must have been dreaming when she thought she felt Jet's light kiss on her forehead.

Chapter Eight

"Mother, why are you here?" A dismayed Jet queried.

Mignon Trideaux looked at her son as if he was dense and not very bright. "The ball." Don't tell me that you've forgotten." The Fundraiser Ball is next week."

"Oh that." He had actually forgotten that he was hosting a fundraiser ball for U.S. Senator, Jonathan Adams, Sr. who was running for the office of governor of the state. "But Mother, that still doesn't answer my question." Why are you here?"

His mother rolled her eyes heavenward. "I'm here to help of course." You did ask for my help, some time ago. "Jet do I need to remind you of the importance of this event.." Who knows, we might be hosting an event that will insure the election of the first African American to be elected governor of this state." I think I should stay here, so that I can make sure everything is perfect."

"Un, huh." Jet gave his mother a look of incredulity. He knew the ball was only a small factor in his mother's percipitate visit. For the most part, she was there to thwart his romance with Adele.

Adele. He had hoped that he would get a chance to talk to her that morning before he went to the office. He had rushed to answf'lr the door in hope of it being Adele only to find his meddlesome mother on his doorsteps at eight in the morning. *Damn!* His letting his desire makhim lose control was a mistake. But embarassing Adele was unforgiveable. He still found it difficult to believed his callous treatment of her feelings. He had always prided himself on being a man of his word. The instant he had felt the evidence of Adele's virginity he had known that he hadn't kept his promise.

Though he had left Adele's maidenhead intact, he had made love to her. He knew her intimately. It was the knowledge that he had not kept his promise to her father that had fed his anger. Somehow he had to make Adele understand that his anger had not been aimed at her but himself.

Adele had found it impossible to harness enough courage to face Jet that morning. Instead of going to his house, she had headed for the stables to visit Sangfroid. She really needed to talk to her best friend, to clear the cobwebs. She was very confused about what had happened. Jet had been so attentive and loving. She had actually began to believe just maybe he loved her. Then his sudden change.

Sangfroid's ears perked up the instant he saw Adele. His beautiful horse eyes serenely followed Adele as she grabbed a carrot from a nearby basket and brought it to him.

"If only all the males in my life were so easy to please." Sangfroid I've made such a mess of everything." Adele told the horse who greedily ate the carrot she had given him. As Adele watched Sangfroid gobble up another carrot, the memory of Jet's unbirdled lovemaking and her wanton response caused an aching sliver of excitement to streak through her. It had been wonderful, beautiful. Jet's wild and hot kisses had consumed her, —possessed her. She wondered if any other man could make her feel the··things Jet had made her feel.

How could something so beautiful tum so ugly? Had what she done been so outrageous? She wasn't the first woman to seduce a man, and she defintely wouldn't be the last. Jet's anger at her had been superfluous. Jet had to take some responsibility in what had happened, also. Wasn't he the one who had taken her to that damnable office. Afterward, he had ordered her to get dressed as if he hadn't been the one to undress her in the first place. The more Adele moulded over the incident, the angrier she became. Soon, her initial embarassment was replaced by outrage.

"You know what, Sangfroid, I'm going to stop cowarding out here in the stables and march right up there and let Jacques Entione Trideaux know that he can't treat me this way and expect me to accept it with out comment."

"I see you haven't changed, despite your notoriety." Mr. Thiboudeaux chuckled behind her. "You still talk to that horse like he's a person."

"Oh that's because he's a good listener and he has a lot of good horse sense." Adele joked.

Mr. Thiboudeaux laughed. "And you still keep me laughing., too." "But seriously, I saw you on the national news last night and you sure looked pretty. A real lady. That's what you looked like.

To bad, I didn't remember to act like a lady. Adele thought drily.

You getting to be such a lady, guess I'm gonna have to start calling you Miss Adele."

"Don't you even think it, Mr. Thiboudeaux. We're practically family, remember we're related by love of horses."

Mr. Thiboudaux nodded in agreement and laughed heartily. "Well, Miss, I mean Adele, I still say you're turning out to be some lady." "You know something else, I bet Mr. Trideaux thinks so too."

"Well, you would lose" Adele mumbled under her breath.

Once Adele entered the house she began a room to room search on the first floor for Jet. He usually didn't leave for his office until about 8:30. She was sure she would find him home. She was determined to tell him just how awful he had made her feel. She heard movement in the study. She rushed in thinking to find Jet but found Mignon Trideaux, instead. The obvious ire of Jet's mother knocked the wind out of Adele's sails.

"What are you doing in my son's house?" "I work here. I'm the housekeeper." "Since when?"

"A few days ago." "Where's Miss Aucoin?"

"In Barbadoes nursing her very ill sister." Adele replied as calmly as she could.

Mignon Trideaux, assessed Adele with cool disdain. "I don't believe you. "Good gracious, just look at you. "You're dressed to work in the stables, not run a house such as this." "My son would never do something so foolish as to hire someone like you to run his house at a time like this!"

Adele looked down at the faded overalls and white long sleeve tee shirt she was wearing. Her back stiffen proudly. "I'm clean, aren't I?"

"Young lady I don't care if you are in my son's mentor program, any more insolence from you and I will fire you in an instant".

"Mrs. Trideaux, I don't mean any disrespect, but I was hired by Jet, and he and only he can fire me."

God, she had came there expecting to find Jet, instead, she had to deal with Jet's Atilla the Hun mother who at that moment looked as if she could easily wring Adele's neck. She may have, if the phone hadn't rung and she made sure she was the one, not Adele to answer it.

When Adele had not shown up for work, Jet concluded that she most likely would be at the stables visiting with Sangfroid.

"She left just, a little while ago, heading your way. I don't see how you missed her." Mr. Thiboudeaux told Jet.

"I must have missed her, when I went to the back garage to get the truck." He concluded. Mon Dieu. He had to get back up to the house. The last thing that Adele needed was to have to contend with his mother.

Adele couldn't believe it when Mignon Trideaux handed her the phone and said. "It's for you".

"My name is Jonathan Adams Jr." "We met briefly last night at Jet's party." The voice at the other end told a mystified Adele. "I inquired about you to Mrs. Trideaux after you and Jet had gone. She said that you were in Jet's mentor program and Jet was called away on urgent business and he was going to see to you getting back home.

So that's how Mignon Trideaux had explained her presence at the party with Jet. No way was she about to let her party guests think that her precious son would deign to get involved with the stable help. Adele had thought she couldn't feel any more miserable.

"Adele, I would like to come out to see you." Maybe we could go out to dinner, or something. "Would that be okay?" I wondered."

Adele was flabbergasted. She couldn't believe it. She was actualy being asked out on a date by no less than a U.S. Senators' son. And she recalled from her brief introduction to him, he was really good looking. But she hadn't really cared because she had eyes only for Jet. Maybe it was time that changed. Maybe it was time she stopped throwing herself at a man who didn't think she was good enough to make love to.

"Adeles voice seemed foreign to her as she replied. "I think that would be nice. "When would you like to come out here?"

"How about tonight?" He asked eagerly.

"Tonight would be fine." She answered without thinking. She didn't want to ponder what she was doing. She might change her mind.

"That's great." I'll be there around six, if you tell me how to get there."

Like a person who has been caught in a very thick fog and has begun to find his way out, Adele was at first disoriented. She made a couple of attempts at directing him from New Orleans to her house. On the third try, she was finally able to give coherent directions.

When Jet had walked into the study. Adele was on the phone and her back was to the door. His mother had immediately halted his progress toward Adele and shushed him. She gleefully and quickly explained in hush tones to her son how Jonathan Adams, Jr. had been quite impressed by his brief encounter with Adele and had tracked her down.

His mother faded into the background. Jet could no longer hear her insidious pratter. All he could hear was Adele voice accepting a date with another man, a man that was closer to her age. Maybe his insensate behavior to Adele the night before had dispelled her of the notion that she was in love with him. He knew it was better that it happened now, than later. However that didn't make it hurt any less. Hurt? Hell, he was dying. Without making Adele aware of his presence he left.

This is better than anything I could have cooked up for the little golddigging upstart. Mignon Trideaux thought maliciously. She would soon be out of Jet's life. But first she had to get her out of Jet's house.

Adele buried herself in housework and the preparation of lunch and supper. Most of all she made sure she stayed clear of Mignon Trideaux which wasn't too difficult since the woman spent most of the day in the study on the phone.

Adele could lose herself in her cooking almost as easily as she could lose herself in her writing. She didn't want to think about her date with a total stranger that evening or that Jet was obviously upset with her still. Moreover, she wanted to prove to Mignon Trideaux that she was capable. For lunch Adele decided to prepare a simple tossed salad, savory steaks, roasted herb potatoes, and steamed green beans almondine and for dessert, she had whipped up a heavenly concoction called Fruit Clouds which was fruit served on a bed of cream cheese mixture. Each day, Adele, tried new and creative ways to serve Jet fresh fruit. She knew it was good for his ulcer.

Adele was thinly slicing the succulent steaks when Mignon Trideaux decided to check upon her.

"Something smells awfully good in here." She walked about the large kitchen, sniffing and peering into pots. When she came to the rolled dough on the chefs table, she did a double take. "You can actually roll dough?" She looked at Adele as if she was seeing her for the very first time.

"My mama taught me how to cook pastries when I was very young."

You're still very young. Mignon was reminded of one the many reasons this girl was wrong for Jet. "Why are you rolling dough?"

"This dough is for tonight's baked cream cheese appetizer." "That's sounds very ambitious."

"Not really, I've prepared it before." Mignon looked surprised.

Adele had to smile. *Just wait until you taste my cooking.*

"Mrs. Trideaux, would you like your lunch in the dinning room or the breakfast nook? The woman was making Adele nervous. She wanted her out ofher . . . Jet's kitchen as soon as possible. The woman's irksome scrutiny might cause her to make an error in preparing that evenings supper of chicken cordon blu, broccoli and rice with walnuts and asparagus in anchovy sauce. There was a zillion ways she could blow that meal, if she wasn't in top form. "Do you want me to serve your lunch in the dinning room or the breakfast nook." Adele asked again. Then crossed her flour covered fingers behind her back. Maybe Mignon Trideaux would take the hint and get out of the kitchen.

Mignon wondered if the child knew how to set a proper table setting. Well, she was about to find out.

"The dinning room." It's very serene in there. Her eyes fell on Adele briefly and then did a final survey of the large kitchen with all its shiny utensils, most which were foreign to her. She felt inadequate. She didn't like that feeling at all. But still she lingered.

"I need to get my wits about me. She explained in a slightly flustered tone. It was something about this girl that she couldn't quite pin down, a certain familiarity. And the more she came in contact with her the more uneasy she became.

"It's been one hectic morning." Mignon continued. Besides, there's far to much light in the breakfast nook for my comfort." Good gracious, I would have to wear a sun hat and sun screen in that place.

Adele knew it was mean of her to think it, but she couldn't help but think, *"A little sunlight might darkened your flawless cafe au lait complexion. And that just wouldn't do at all, would it Mrs. Trideaux?*

Adele thought about how Jet loved eating in the sunny breakfast nook. Dear God, what have I done?" The anquished query vibrated in her mind. She loved Jet. Nothing was ever going to change that. Not even his acting the jerk. But she would deal with that problem later. Right now she had to deal with making sure she set that table correctly for Mignon Trideaux. The woman was probably just waiting for her to screw up.

For Jet, she usually set a simple place setting for dinner. However, she knew she would have to go the whole nine yards for Mignon Trideaux. God, please let her leave so that I can take a quick refresher from the etiquette book. Adele prayed a fervent silent prayer. God must have been listening. At that very instant, the phone rang and Mignon rushed to answer it.

Adele went all out. She chilled red wine to go with the lunch. For medicimal purposes, Jet usually had a glass of wine with his lunch or his supper. He said it relaxed the muscles in his stomach. Where was Jet, anyway? He should've been home for lunch by then. Well, he was probably still avoiding her, Adele thought. Too bad, he didn't know that he didn't have to be concerned about her lovesick decorum, anymore.

Though Adele used the best dinnerware and flatware and not china and silver, she used a intricate place setting that included several forks, spoons, knives and glasses. The surprised and outdone look on Mignon Trideaux's face when she sat down was priceless. Adele gave a silent thanks.

A little while later, Adele checked in to see if Jet had shown up. He had not. "Do you need anything, Mrs. Trideaux?"

Mignon Trideaux paused from eating and stared at Adele as if she was seeing her for the first time. "This tastes really wonderful." Mignon admitted grudgingly. "I don't think I've ever known green beans to taste this good. What did you do?

"I steamed them in chicken flavored bouillon and crushed almonds. Adele answered slowly. She couldn't believe that she had actually done something that pleased Mignon Trideaux.

Mignon took a bite of the last slice of steak. Her eyes rolled heavenward as she savored it. She finally swallowed then looked at Adele with dawning admiration. "You're quite the cook." She told a beaming Adele. For the first time, she gave Adele what appeared to be a genuine smile.

She not's so bad after all. Adele thought.

"I've been thinking, Adele. Since you such a wiz in the kitchen and all, how would you like to help prepare the hors d' euvres for the upcoming fundraiser ball for Senator Adams?

Adele's heart sank. So that was it. That's why she began treating me like I was a human—being. Adele thought miserably. Nothing had changed. Even though the Senator's son was interested in Adele, Mignon Trideaux still didn't deem her fit to attend the ball. She had regaled Adele to the kitchen.

Noticing Adele's not so thrilled expression, she quickly added. "Of course, you'll be paid extra for your help."

Adele first instinct was to say no. But then she though about what fun it would be to try out some food creations she had been dying to prepare.

"I'll do it. If you will allow me to choose the foods to be served.

Mignon hesitated for a moment. "That'll be fine. But you must make sure I've approved the menu.

"Will do." Adele promised.

After setting the table for two in a fine china and crystal that was delegated for regular dinners, Adele set into place everything for Jet and his mother, including the chilled white wine and the cream cheese appetizer and its accompanying grapes and apple slices. The main course and side dishes were in silver warmers on the buffet. Jet and his mother could serve themselves. She had only a little over an hour to get ready for her date with Jonathan Adams, Jr.

When Adele told her parents that Jonathan Adams, Jr. was coming by and was going to take her out to dinner. They were as floored by the news as she had been when he had asked her. Quickly recovering from his initial shock, Zechariah Baychan was particularly pleased by the news. He respected Jonathan Adams, Sr.'s record as a U.S. senator, and thought that he would be make a good governor. Jonathan Adams, Jr., had often campaigned for his father. And from what he had seen of him on television he seemed to be a young man that was going places himself.

"So my baby gal's going to be dating Jonathan Adams, Jr. Adele shared a special look with her mother.

"Boy I bet all the folks in these parts gonna really be envious of the Baychans for a change." Her daddy bragged proudly.

"Daddy before you go out spreading the news, let's see how this date goes." Adele sighed.

Zechariah studied his beautiful daughter for a moment. She didn't seem too excited about going out with the Adams fellow. Not nearly as excited when she had "Adele, you don't still have the foolish notion that you're in love with Jet Trideaux do ya?"

Cause if you do, I tell you right now, get it out of ya head. You will never have a chance of a life with 'em. You might have a chance with this Adams fellow because his daddy's from a different kinda stock than the Trideauxs. "Born poor he was. And he pulled himself up and made something of himself."

"Daddy believe me, I know where I stand with Jet."

Her father eyed her suspiciously. "Jet didn't take advantage ofya' on your trip to New Orleans, did he?

"No daddy." Jet didn't take advantage of me. Her daddy would probably be ashamed, if he knew of her outrageous behavior.

Adele turned to her Mama, who was unusually quiet. "Mama,

Mamma, I need you to help me get ready." Adele panted. I've only got an hour to get dressed! Adele did her best to sound excited.

Adele had always thought her mother to be the most beautiful woman on earth, not only physically but spirtually as well. Through all the hardships they had endured, her mother had managed to maintain her physical beauty and serene demeanor. Adele had always wished that she could be as patient as her mother. However, most people said that Adele was the spitting image of her mother though Adele was not as dark skinned as her mother. Albeit, they both had long thick and curly hair, and the same chocolate brown eyes.

"Adele you can't throw me off as easily as you can your daddy." "You're as much in love with Jet Trideaux as you ever was." Her mother told her as she rummaged through Adele's closet.

"Well, I don't want to be. Not anymore. Mama I'm so tired oftrying to prove my selfworth to others. Adele anquished. It's hell Mama. And I refuse to reinvent myself to become someone that Jet might consider marrying. Fat chance of that anyway.

"So, you going out with another man to get over Jet." "Well, if you truly love Jet, baby it's not going to work. "You won't stop loving Jet, just because you bring another man into the picture. Love doesn't work that way."

"Who's says that I love Jet'?

Lorraine rolled her eyes heavenward.

"Daddy is right. "It's just a crush. Adele insisted. Jacques Trideaux is the type of man that inspires women to have crushes on him. It's about time I get over my silly crush on him.

Lorraine gave her melodramatic daughter an indulgent smile as she held up a yellow dress for her inspection. Receiving a staunch negative, she continued her search of the stuffed closet.

"Do you ever throw anything away, baby?" Why are you still holding on to this old thing?" She asked, showing Adele a dress wrapped in a clear plastic garment bag. I have a mind to throw this thing in the garbage.

"Mama, don't you dare!" Adele cried. She jumped up from her perched position on her bed and grabbed the garment. "Mama, that's the dress I was wearing the first time I saw Jet. "I rather cut off an arm than get rid of that dress.

"Un huh". Her mother laughed. "Seems to me, those are pretty strong sentiments for a woman who is ready to move on."

Adele gave her mother an impish smile. "You don't expect me to let go of Jet cold turkey, do you?" After all, he's been my every thought, my every desire since that first day."

"I know baby." Believe me, I know. She laughed. "What possessed you to put on this old evening gown that day?'

"Silliness." That's all. I was reading about parties and rich people during the Civil War era, and I guess I just wanted to get a feeling of what that was like for someone like Scarlett O'Hara."

"Well, I was off cleaning house that day for one of the descendants of the Scarlet 0' Haras of the south." That was our reality. "That dress is so old you would think that it came from the 1850s, the 1950s at the least. Somebody gave it to me, a long time ago. Who it was I can't remember. Her forehead furrowed. I just can't remember. But the dress is of no importance. Life for us was very different back then. We had so little. "But you never complained. Filled with warmth and pride, Lorraine Baychans eyes fell on her daughter.

"You use to live in this world of make believe Adele." I worried about you." Then I started finding stories that you had written and I knew you were putting that vivid imagination of yours to good use."

Adele's eyes welled with tears when she looked at her mother. "It is because of you Mama that I have such an imagination. You were the one that introduced me to the world of books. "I use to hide my stories because I was ashamed of some of the things that I wrote." I was afraid that my writings reflected too much of my inner longings." And if someone read my stories then I would be stripped bare, left defenseless. God, she had felt that way when Jet had abruptly rejected what she had been so willing to give him.

Noticing the forlomess that had descended on her daughter, Lorraine queried gently. "Honey is there something you want or need to tell your Mama?

No. Adele shook her head emphatically. She couldn't tell her mother. It was too painful and embarassing.

"Really Mama." Adele forced a lightness into her tone so that her mother wouldn't pry any further. I'm becoming dispondent, that's all. I don't have a decent thing to wear."

"You could wear the black dress you wore last night.

Adele rolled her eyes in mock horror. "Mother, surely you jest." I can't let Jonathan see me in the same dress. "It would be akin to barbarism." Her mother laughed. Adele you and your melodramatics you remind me of my sister Nadine." She shooked her head and was pensive for a moment.

"Mama, you hardly ever mention Aunt Nadine moreless talk about her. Why is that?"

To painful I guess. She died many years ago. You're like her in many ways. You also walk to a different drum. Yes, you're a lot like your Aunt Nadine, beautiful, talented and as kind as the day is long." Most people didn't notice the kind part about Nadine. She stopped talking and help up a dress for Adele's inspection.

"I look hideous in purple." Adele told.

Moments later, Lorraine shrieked in a tone synomymous to her daughter's. "I've got it." She pulled a deep sage crepe sheath dress and its matching bolero jacket from the closet. "How about this dress that you wore to our church's homecoming celebration earlier this month. It's new.

"That would be okay, if it didn't have that potato salad stain." Adele had been on the food serving committe as usual. Someone had spilled part of their meal on her which was a usual occurrence, also.

"You're the cook around here, but remember I am the expert laundress."

I have a home dry cleaning kit. And I'll have this dress as right as rain in a jiffY." Her mother promised.

Her mother was true to her promised. Forty-five minutes later, Adele put the finishing touch to her ensemble. She tied her thick mane back with a matching green scarf.

Jonathan Adams, Jr. was true to his word. He arrived promptly at SIX. He was even more handsome than Adele had recalled. He was just as handsome as Jet maybe even moreso. He was tall like Jet, but as dark as hickory roast coffee. The dark sports jacket and matching slacks he wore fit him as if they were tailored. When he flashed his winning smile, dimples formed. He was defintely a heart throb. After introducing himself to her parents, Jonathan took a seat on the livingroom couch and chat with her parents, briefly. He looked at his watch and said that they had to get going if they were to make their seven o'clock dinner reservation in Baton Rouge.

The heart throb persona continued. He opened the door to his shiny black BMW and helped Adele in like a true gentleman. On the drive to the restaraunt, he and Adele got to know each other. Adele learned that he had just finished law school and was studying to take the state bar. And that he would probably go into politics one day like his father. He was easy to talk too, and he put Adele right at ease. She liked him.

"You are a lovely young woman, Adele." You're smart, gifted and just downright fine." He laughed boyishly. I can see why Jet Trideaux, is so obviously in love with you."

Adele who was struggling with her lobster and wishing immensely that she had not let Jonathan talk her into trying the obstinate crustacean, dropped the whatchamagadget she was trying to use. "What did you say?"

"I said He started then laughed. "You heard me." "I don't understand."

"I do. "Who can blame Jet. It's easy enough to understand, he said leaning toward Adele. "I would fall for you myself, ifI was interested in your gender." He laughed as Adele took a large gulp of ice water.

"But, why did you ask me out?" Adele sputtered.

"Let's just said, I decided to do a good deed, and have a little fun too."
"I don't like being the butt of someone's silly joke." Adele's eyes flashed angrily. She had thought him to be a gentleman. He was having fun at her expense.

"Adele, I would never have fun at your expense." He said, as if reading her thoughts.

"It's that snooty Mignon Trideaux, in which my fun is aimed."

"I could tell by the way she and that equally snobbish Paulette Joseph were huddled together at the party that they were plotting to come between you and Jet."

"You're wrong about that." There's nothing for them to come between where Jet and I are concerned." I'm just one of Jet's good deed projects.

"You love Jet don't you?"

"Maybe."

"Don't you know?" Shouldn't a woman know whether or not she loves a man?"

"If we were talking about your ordinary man, yes. But Jet's different. I'm sure he makes any woman that he comes into contact with feel as I do. He's every woman's fantasy. But a fantasy isn't the basis of true love. At least, I don't think so."

"So, what is it that you want from Jet?"

Adele answered without hesitation. "I want him to be the first. The first man to make love to me."

Lonny coughed and then grabbed his water and gulped half of it down. He studied Adele long and hard. Then he said, "you have all the attributes. I don't see what the problem is. "You shouldn't have any problem seducing any man, even Jet."

"Believe it or not, I've been fighting a losing battle."

"Well, you're not fighting alone now, he whispered. You have me in your comer."

"Here's the plan." He leaned toward Adele. In a hushed conspiratory voice, he told her. "No man wants a woman that doesn't have at least one other admirer besides himself." Especially a man like Jet." He thrives on competition." So I'm going to be the competition."

"So you're going to help me make Jet jealous." "That's the plan."

Adele eyed him suspiciously. "What are you getting out of this?" "Besides, making Mignon's life a bit uncomfortable, which is incentive enough, I would help my father also", he told her, his voice dropping even lower. "In this early stage of my daddy's bid for governor, I don't want even a hint of family scandal to emerge. It could hurt his chances of getting the support he needs."

"People have gone beyond that." Adele leaned closer to ensure that her words wouldn't be heard by nearby dinners. They wouldn't let your sexual preference stop them from donating money to your fathers campaign."

"Yes, they would. "I am afraid." "That's why, on the night of the ball, I want all the movers and shakers of the Democratic party of Louisiana to see me walk in with you on my arm."

"Why, Mr. Adams, are you asking lit' ol' me to the ball?" Adele batted her eyelids, saucily.

"I do believe I am, Miss Adele." "I do believe I am."

Then they both broke into peels of laughter. They caused the other dinners to pause and stare and then to look at each other as if to say, were we ever that young and that muchhhh in love.

But seriously, we will kill two birds with one stone." Jonathan managed to say, after his laughter had abated. "We will help my Daddy get elected and make Jet realize he would be a fool to let you get away from him."

"Partners." They agreed together and clasped hands across the table Jet had hardly touched the wonderful meal Adele had prepared for his dinner. All he could think about was that Adele was out on a date. He had excused himself from his mother's company and gone into his study. Since Sangfroid's win, he had beefed up security on the ranch. He pondered whether or not he should have one of his security specialists follow Adele and young Adams. He'd snatched up his phone several times to do so, then slammed it down. The chaotic savagery of his thoughts had halted him. He couldn't tell his security specialists to follow Adele and her date and kill Adams if he so much as kissed Adele. That was madness. But then he was insane with jealousy.

The next morning Adele, got up at the crack of dawn. She had a renewed sense of purpose. Jonny, her newly found friend, had convinced her that her plan had a fighting chance. All she had to do was play her cards right.

She visited her old friend, Sangfroid. Then she headed to work. At seven a.m., she was busily preparing breakfast for Jet and his mother. She sang as she set the table.

Adele's sweet litany was the sound that met Jet as he trudged down the stairs. He had a headache. He had probably sleep two hours at most.

"Good morning, Jet. She spoke brightly as he eased down into an end chair.

He grunted.

"Doesn't seem like you're feeling so hot this morning. "But I've got just the thing that will perk you right up". Adele said in a tone sweeter than the platter of honey glazed blackberry sconces she set in front of him.

He didn't want to, but he couldn't help himself. Jet found himself staring at Adele. She was almost radiant. There was a special sparkle in her eyes. A sliver of jealsousy slithered through him. Had Adams caused Adele's apparent happiness?"

As soon as Mignon Trideaux had seated herself in the other end chair, Adele dropped her bombshell. "Mrs. Trideaux, I am afraid I will not be able to help serve during the ball." Jonny Adams asked me to be his date for that night. "Of course, I will prepare all the hors-d'oeuvre. I just won't be able to help serve them, that's all."

Jet glared down the table at his mother who squirmed uneasily, but had not looked in his direction. He couldn't believe she had actually asked Adele to serve at the ball. He was tom between the desire to be a respectful and loving son and the urge to ask his mother to leave his home. He knew it had not been easy for his mother but this was a bit too malicious.

"Adele you don't have to prepare the food for the ball." Mother will hire caterers like she usually does." He scowled in his mother's direction who at the time seemed to be paying an awful lot of attention to her plate.

"But Jet, its something I really would like to do." Adele protested. "You know how I love to create in the kitchen." Let me do this." "Pretty please." Adele pleaded playfully.

Jet relented. "Fine, do what you want." You usually do, anyway."

The note of recrimination in Jet's tone renewed Mignon's hope that all would go as planned. Her son was already beginning to see just how shallow this girl was.

The ball was all everybody in St. Pierre were talking about. Mignon Trideaux had even bought air time on local radio and television stations to discuss the ball. It was being billed as the event. Local churches were raising the required two thousand dollars so that they could send their minister and his wife. They didn't want to miss out on what they felt was a historic event.

The ballroom at Fiveforks was a rectangle area with dimensions of 60 by 80 feet. Even with the added addition of a stage that had been set up for the muscians, it could easily hold a hundred dancing couples.

When Adele walked into the empty ballroom, as usual, she was overwhelmed by the enormity of the place. The polished wood floor, the giant marble fireplaces and the opulent crystal chandeliers gave the place a fairytale quality. It was hard for her to connect the man that she loved to the one that had built such a house. It was rumored that the house had casted over twenty million dollars to build. A man who could spend that kind of money on a house was incongruent to the man that teased her until he made her so mad she could throw something at him, or the man who made her heart leap with joy whenever he smiled at her or the man who made her body and soul bum with passion whenever he gave her one of his smouldering looks. How had she managed to get so close to Jet. The memory of what his lips and hands had felt like on her body caused pleasure sweet and thick to slowly spread through her. He had kissed her as if he couldn't get enough. She shivered and clasped her arms about herself as if to bind the pleasure so that it could not escape. Maybe Jonny was right.

Could it be that Jet actually loved her?

Arms still clasped about herself, Adele began to sway to an imaginary waltz. She imagined that the beautiful ballroom was filled with dancing couples attired in formal evening clothes swirling about her as she danced with Jet. As she moved she let the imaginary music pull her into a magical realm. Her feet moved faster, faster, and faster. She no longer felt the floor beneath her feet. Jet was holding her and he was smiling, and she was floating on clouds of love.

Jet came to the ballroom to give the newly built stage his personal inspection. The vision of Adele dancing checked his progress into the room. Jet stood in the opened doorway and watched Adele dance. His heart was filled with love and humility. He remembered the first time he had seen her dance. She'd been in the stables was using a bam broom for a dancing partner. Like now, he had been enthralled by the grace and beauty in which she danced. But most of all he had been humbled. This little snip of a girl had the uncanny ability to transcend hardship and mundaness and created her own little world of beauty. Adele had the ability to create imaginary beauty that spilled over into reality. She made things happen. She moved people to action. He had watched her dance and had known that he wanted to be her dancing partner throughout life. He had taken private dancing lessons so that he would not disappoint her when he finally did dance with her. Adele's special creative powers didn't stop with her dancing. The meals that she managed to whip up, that accomodated his bland diet, were magical. And when she wrote, she created characters whose love transcended all the barriers and problems that stood between them. From the few excerpts he read of her novel, he ascertained that she was basically writing about herself and him. She had placed them in a historical setting. Still he wondered if the love she felt for him was real or was it just part of a school girl fantasy that she would soon outgrow or had already outgrown.

"Jet!"

He shushed his mother. He didn't want Adele to know that he had been watching her dance.

"The people who are to polish and buff the ballroom floor are on the phone, Mignon said in a now hush tone." They need further directions. "You know I don't know anything about this area." Talk to them. She ordered and gave him the cellular receiver.

While Jet was giving directions, she peeped into the ballroom. She then turned to Jet; smirked and then shook her head.

"Mother your displeasure is quite obvious." Jet said as he handed her the phone. "But I swear, Mama. If you say one mean thing to Adele, if you do another underhanded thing to Adele, I will personally pack your things and take you back to New Orleans.

"What I've got to say, it's for you. Mignon decided she would change her tactics. "Jet you're fooling yourself. "Look at her. She was tempted to hiss but softened her tone. She's a lovely girl and all. But do you think a butterfly such as she will be able to endure the rigorous responsibilities of being Mrs. Jacques Trideaux. She's too delicate Jet. It will destroy her. If you truly love this girl, you will come to realize that too."

"Mother your little lecture is superfluous." You forget Adele has a date for the ball and that date is not me." Jet gave his mother a perfunctory kiss on the cheek. "Mother I am sure there's more you want to say, but I have to get to the office."

Mignon stared after her son. He's was right. There was lots more she wanted to say and would say as soon as she had all the facts about this girl who had so obviously bewithched her son. Like father like son, she thought bitterly.

Adele's moment on the ballroom dance floor was her last quiet moment. The rest of the week she was involved in a flurry of activities. First she'd determined the divers hors d'oeuvres she would prepare for the ball. Having done that she had to prepare a supply list. This was the most difficult part. She had never prepared hor d'oeuvres for so many people. Then she had to contact various suppliers to determined ifthey had in stock some of the things needed. Then she went grocery shopping. It was exhilerating. Then the day before the ball the catering company that was to serve at the ball sent three assistants to help Adele prepare the hor d' oeuvres. They worked far into the evening getting everything set up so that they could bring it all together the next day.

It was almost nine o'clock in the evening when Jet strolled into the kitchen looking as if he had just stepped off the cover of Gentlemen's Quarterly. Adele hadn't seen him in days. He been out of state on some urgent business. As usual Adele's wayward heart raced upon sight of him. With hands that had became suddenly unsteady, Adele continued shaking the sifter of flour onto the crust she was rolling.

After he had greeted Adele and her three, by then, almost catatonic helpers, Jet meandered about the large kitchen for a few moments, looking, and stopping to sample a canape or a cracker and a dip here and there.

"You done a great job Adele. He said finally. "Everything looks and tastes great."

"This is only part of what's going to be served." The easily perishables such as the baked stuffed shrimp and clams will be prepared tomorrow.

"What are these?" He asked.

"They're curried chicken puffs."

"They look delicious, but I better not try one. Probably to spicy."

"Probably." Adele nodded in agreement. Then she remembered.

She dropped the sifter and rushed pass Jet into the pantry to the large industrial size refrigerator where they had stored many of the hors d' oeuvres.

"Try this." She offered him a mini fruit cheese tart. Adele had given him a banana/strawberry one. A warm feeling of self-pride washed over her as she watched Jet bite into the flaky curst of the tiny tart with obvious delight.

When he had finished, he said. "That tart was out of this world. "Adele if you weren't covered from head to toe with flour, I would hug you." His dark eyes danced with laughter.

For the first time, Adele noticed that she was a mess.

"See you at the ball milady." He blew a kiss to a flustered Adele. He gave the three catatonic helpers a wink and he swaggered out of the kitchen.

Jet was gone a full minute before the helpers regained their ability to speak. Adele wished they hadn't. They talked about nothing else but Jet up until the time they called it a day at ten o' clock.

Later, an exhausted Adele had taken a quick shower and crawled into her bed. As she fell asleep the favorite phrase of the helpers vibrated in her head. "The Prince ofthe Creoles" is giving a ball."

CHAPTER NINE

"Adele awaken with but one thought on the morning of the ball—revenge. So, Jet had found her messy appearance amusing. Well, she would have the last laugh. When she walked into the ball that evening on Jonny's arm, looking resplendent, she would have her revenge. She would have a revenge that would be sweeter than the fruit tarts that Jet loved. She would have revenge on Jet for always amusing himself at her expense, and she would have her revenge on Mignon Trideaux for always looking down her aquiline nose at her. Most of all, she would have her revenge on the damnable lady in waiting, Paulette Joseph.

Adele had found the perfect gown at, of all places, a bridal shop. With the alterations her mom had made, the strapless dress fit Adele as if he had been especially tailored for her. That illusion was supported by the gowns dazzling milk chocolate color which matched Adele eyes perfectly. The shimmering silk material of the gown and its matching wrap had an ethereal quality. Adele had decided to ballast it with a multi-strand necklace of sparkling glass crystals on nearly invinsible wire. The necklace was accompanied by a matching set oflarge dangling earrings and the multi-strand braclet. The necklace was not only heavy in weight it was heavy in price as well. To pay for it, Adele had depleted the rest of the twenty-thousand she had won at the horserace.

Adele knew the money had been well spent by Jonny's initial reaction that evening. When she walked into their living room to greet him, he stood slowly like a man in a daze.

"Have mercy." He drolled. In a more serious tone, he added. Adele you look spectacular."

After her dad had taken a dozen pictures or more of Adele and her date, Adele kissed her beaming mother and started out for the ball. Before Adele gingerly settled down into Jonny's BMW she gave a wave to her parents who stood watching from the porch of their double-wide mobile home.

Long after Zach had gone inside, Lorraine Baychan remained on the porch. She was reflecting on how much Adele had changed in the past three years. Adele had gone from a beautiful outcast who lived in a world of books and music to a self-assured young lady who was being escorted to a society ball by the son of a U.S. Senator. What had brought about this miracle could be sumed up in three letters—Jet. From the moment, Jet had entered their lives things had gotten better and better. His sensitive treatment of lovesick Adele had made her come out of her cacoon. He had given her a parttime job that she loved and put her in his mentor program. But most importantly, he had treated her like the unique and lovely girl that she was. Under his kind guidance, Adele had blossomed. A mother's instinct told her that what Adele felt for Jet was more than just a school girl crush. An icy sliver of anxiety streaked through her. She shivered. The depth of Adele's love for Jet made Lorraine afraid. Adele was going to get hurt. Zach was right. Men like Jet didn't marry poor girls like Adele, especially dark-skinned ones.

Adele wanted her entrance to the ball to be nothing short of spectacular as well. She had pondered it most of the day. She decided it was best that Jonny and she should use the southside entrance to the ballroom. Fiveforks was built on a large bluff that Jet had created with the transport of thousands of tons of dirt. There was a drive way that circled the hill in which the house was situated. On the south end of the house, little cobble stone steps built into the hillside ascended to the terrace that was outside the ballroom.

After Jonny had helped her from the car, Adele looked upward toward the ballroom. She shivered and pulled her wrap tightly about her bared shoulders.

"Adele, you are a winner ifl ever saw one. You don't have to be nervous. Remember, you out to seduce Louisiana's most eligible bachelor. Jonny reminded her of purpose." He crooked his arm and she grasped it.

As they ascended the steps, Adele took deep breaths. Where had all her bravado gone?.

When Jonny and she stood at the threshold of the double plated glass doors of the ballroom, they open as if by magic. Adele was too dazzled by the sight before her to notice the two door attendants. She was looking down the long corridor of chandeliers that hung over the heads of the guests. There was a den of talk. Everyone was milling about talking.

"There're my parents." Jonny whispered in her ear. As they made their progress toward them a hush fell over the ballroom. Adele didn't know whether to attribute the sudden quiet to the arrival of the guest of honor's son and his date or to her appearance. But she hoped that she looked that damn good!

"Study girl. Jonny said without losing his smile. "They can't take their eyes off of you. "Walk as if you been doing this all your life." He told her.

Adele did her damest to do so. However, Adele almost lost it when she spotted Paulette chatting with Mignon Trideaux up near the stage.

Sensings her tension, Jonny reminded Adele. "Remember, Jet is the prize. "Keep your eyes on the prize."

Jet was on his cellular talking to his late lead musician when Adele arrived. He had designed that ballroom as a tribute to her. Mon Dieu. She lived up to it and more. Dazzling. He was dazzled. As she walked, the full skirt of her gown made her appear to glide, across the shiny floor, her jewelry was caught by the lights of the myriad chandeliers and that light was reflected back to her heart shaped face. Her riotously thick hair had been tamed for the evening. It was pulled backward and hung down her back in a luxurious ponytail. She was flawless. The dress fit her as if it had been sewn on her. Her strenuous work in the stables had given her the sleek body that allowed her to look great in a strapless gown. The memory of how he'd last seen her, covered in flour, made him smile.

Adele felt like she had walked the longest mile or something. But at last they reached Jonny's parents.

"Jonny, she's even more lovely than I remembered." Maribelle Adams beamed. Come on baby, let me introduce you to some people we know." She took a hapless Adele by the arm and steered her toward of group of important looking people." Jonny has talked about little else but you since the other night. And from what he told me, I think you are a very accomplished young lady." She told Adele as they walked.

As Maribelle introduced Adele to her friends and acquaintences, Adele found herself wishing she could somehow get on the good side of Mignon Trideaux. But that was probably a lost cause.

Then it occurred to Adele that no one was dancing. There was a chamber group on the stage playing Mozart.

"Why isn't anyone dancing?" Adele asked.

"You mean, you haven't heard." Maribelle's eyes glittered with excitement. "Wynton Marsalis is on his way" He's Jet's surprise musician for the evening."

All the hard work, the excitement of her entrance, and now to hear that her favorite jazz musician was playing at the ball, was overwhelming. For a moment, Adele felt dizzy.

"May I have your attention, please." Jet announced from center stage. Hundred of eyes were suddenly focused in his direction." He took a deep breath as if to calm himself" Which added to the suspense. "You all will be pleased to know that Mr. Wynton Marsalis is in the building as I speak"!

"Gales of excitment rent the ballroom. Then there was a roar of thunderous applauses when Wynton walked through the door.

As Wynton walked onto the stage, trumpet in hand, he and Jet exchanged a hearty hug.

"Jet, that handsome rascal, didn't even tell us about this until we arrived."

Maribelle was besides herself with happiness. God, what a success this ball is turning out to be."

Then Wynton started playing. The lights were dimmed. Couples started dancing. Maribelle went off to find the Senator. Suddenly, Jonny was at her side. "Well, lady let's get this show on the road." He told her, reminding her of their objective.

"Jet's heart." She mumbled under her breath as she stepped into Jonny's arms and began swaying slowly to the hypnotic pull of Wynton's serenade. Adele could feel the heat of Jet's eyes bore into her back. "Hold me tighter. She directed Jonny. "Jet's watching."

"Jet is trying hard to look unaffected, but Mignon, look how his eyes are following her every move." It pains me to see Jet make such a fool of himself." Paulette observed.

"This girl is as dangerous as I thought. "That little Lolitta is not interested in Adams in the slightest. Jet is her goal." She's trying to make Jet jealous."

"Well, she is succeeding." Paulette remarked caustically.

Mignon could barely contain her hatred. She felt like marching over to the little mare and grabbing her by the ponytail and dragging her from the ballroom. She would move heaven and earth before she allowed Jet to tie himself to that unsavory creature. She was from bad stock. "Dammit, Paulette. Don't just stand here looking bitter. Do something."

"What would you have me to do? Paulette rolled her eyes."

"Go over and ask Jet to dance." Mignon exasperated. "Paulette do I have to tell you everything?"

"Jet, dance with me." Paulette said a few moments later.

The last thing Jet wanted to do on earth at that moment was to dance with Paulette. But there was no gracious way he could refuse.

The second Jet's eyes left her, Adele knew it. She turned to see what had take his attention from her and Jonny. She was sickened with jealousy by the sight of him dancing with Paulette Joseph. God, what had she expected. Did she really expect Paulette to be a wallflower at this ball. Paulette and Jet moved together in perfect harmony. They looked as if they had planned to be together at the ball. Jet's evening attire, a white dinner jacket and black tuxedo pants coordinated well with Paulette's white evemng gown.

Watching Jet and Paulette on the dance floor, Mignon felt like giving herself a pat on the back for calling Paulette and telling her what Jet would be wearing.

"Jonny, he's dancing with Paulette. Adele cried. "How can he get jealous of us, if he's occupied by her attentions. Jonny, we've got to do something, and do it quickly to make Jet jealous."

And before she realized what he was about to do, Jonny kissed her.

Right there in the middle of the floor with about four-hundred eyes peeled to them, he kissed Adele. It was a sweet short kiss. Adele didn't even have time to react to it. It was the type of kiss given by a young man who was suddenly overwhelmed by the loveliness of the young lady he was dancing with.

Paulette could feel Jet grow as rigid as an English bridle pony. As soon as the song ended, he excused himself by saying he had an urgent call to make to Hawaii and he would have to do it would out distractions. Then he left the ballroom.

"Jonny, I think we went too far." Adele cried.

"Is Jet still dancing with Paulette?", Jonny queried, his eyes sparkling devilishly.

"No. Adele had to admit.

Then we did not go too far. We only did what was necessary."

"I could sense his anger from across the room.," Adele said, biting on her bottom lip. I think the last time I made Jet that angry was the time he caught me horseracing against Anthony on one of his Arabians. Maybe, I should go find him." Adele looked anxiously in the direction in which Jet had gone.

"Let him stew for awhile. Anyway, how would it look, if my date went traipsing behind Jet Trideaux." Jonny reminded Adele of his objective.

So Adele kept dancing with Jonny. And she kept her eyes glued on the door, looking for Jet to return to the ball. But he never did.

"I can't believe Jet would let that little snip of a girl pull his strings like that." Paulette told Mignon. He was fit to be tied, when he left." "Did you see the murderous look he gave Jonny.

Paulette nodded miserably. Even when they had been considered a couple, Jet hadn't shown the least bit of jealousy where she was concerned. "It is best that he did leave. "How would it look if the host had attacked the son of the guest of honor." Mignon exlaimed softly. The scandal that would've been. The very thought made her feel faint for a second.

Paulette we've got to do something, before this situation gets totally out of hand. "We got to make that little Lolitta think that she doesn't stand a chance of ever becoming Mrs. Jacques Trideaux." And she'll be glad to settle for Jonny Adams who obviously has already fallen under her spell."

"Mignon, I know what I have to do and I have just the thing that will do it. I had an intuition that I would need it one day. Paulette suddenly showed some animation.

Mignon gave Paulette a speculative look, but didn't make an inquiry. Whatever Paulette was up to, she wanted to be able to honestly tell Jet she had not known of the duplicity if Paulette was found out.

Adele had enough of trying to save Jonny's face. She had long grown tired of the silly and dangerous game she had been playing with Jonny. She was ready to find Jet and confess. Of course, she wasn't going to divulge Jonny's secret.

Adele decided to make a damage check in the ladies room before she went searching for Jet. She was touching up her lipstick when Paulette Joseph slithered through the door and locked it. Adele fought the invading weariness. She decided she was not going to deal with Paulette's malevolence. It was neither the place nor the time.

"Let me by." Adele demanded softly.

"You not going anywhere." Not until we've talked." Paulette's dark eyes glittered with malice.

"We have nothing to discuss." The weather has been done to death." Adele endeavored to make light of the situation.

"You're wrong about that. "I'm about to rain on your little parade."

Paulette's obvious venom caused Adele's infamous sense of foreboding to rear up.

"I repeat." We have nothing to discuss." Adele made an attempt to get past the taller woman.

"Jet." That's what we have to discuss." But I assure you the conversation will be a very short one. Jet's mine. Always was, always will be."

"If that's true, then why are you threatened?"

"I'm not threaten by you or any of your sort." Jet plays, but he always comes back to me. She gave Adele a sly glare and said. "You poor thing. You really though you meant something to him. "Jet does love to play. You're just another toy to him. She threw back her glossy mane and gave it a superflous little pat. When he marries, it will be to me." Her beautiful dark eyes glittered with malice.

Adele must have shook her head in denial as she stepped back from Paulettes wrath.

"You don't believe me? Paulette gave Adele an insidious little smile. Paulette reminded Adele of a coiled serpent about to strike.

"Here's proof."

Adele took the business card Paulette thrusted at her. It was one of Jet's. Adele gave Paulette a questioning look. "Tum it over."

Adele turned it over. On the back it read. "Paulette, will you marry me?" Jet's infamous scrawl of a signature was at the bottom of the question.

Adele gave the card back to Paulette whose eyes beamed with triumph.

Adele's spirits caved in like a stack of baled hay when one of it bales is suddenly snatched from under. It was too late. Jet had already asked Paulette to marry him. He was forbidden to her forever.

Noting Adele's crestfallen countance, Paulette unlocked the door. She gave Adele one last triumphant glare and said, "You don't have to wonder about my answer to him. It was yes. Paulette did an impish little bounce then she sashayed out.

Chapter Ten

After Paulette's triumphant exit, Adele collapsed against the bathroom wall for a moment. She wondered if it was possible for a mere crush to make her heart ache so. She left the bathroom but she couldn't remember doing so. She was dazed. Numbed. Somehow she ended up in Jet's study. Perhaps unconciously she had sought Jet in some childish hope that he could deny his engagement to Paulette. The study was dark, except for a banker's lamp that threw a greenish glow on the man who appeared to be reading a business report.

What are you doing in here, Adele"? Jet raged softly without looking up from the papers in his hand. Did you come to gloat over the success of your childish game. For the first time he dragged his eyes off the papers and looked at Adele. What happened? You've grown tire of the game, so soon?

Jet's sarcasm invaded the sancutary of numbness that Adele had entered. In his arrogance he had the audacity to be angry at her for being with Jonny when he was engaged to another woman. He was the one playing games. He was playing a very sick game that involved her and the woman he intended to marry one day. Adele wanted to lash out at him call him names even claw his face with the long lacquered nails she had attached to her own short ones. But she decided to use Jet's own jealousy against him.

"What game? I'm not playing a game. "Jonny is a terrific person. He treats me with respect." Her voice quaked. Unshed tears glistened in her eyes.

Jet felt a sliver of remorse. But the memory of her kissing Adams was a raw ache in his—gut. He snarled. "You call that respect. He slammed the stack of papers he was holding down on his desk. "He slobbered all over you before hundreds of people." He lashed out.

No he did not. Adele defended Jonny. *He gave me a very sweet, chaste little kiss. And I liked it.* She had gone too far, Adele realized too late.

Jet's eyes glittered with jealous anger. He was livid.

In an instant, Jet rose and was from behind his desk. He reached her in an instant. He grabbed Adele and crushed her roughly to him. "Tell me Adele, what did you do to him, to make him lose his sense of place? He raged softly against her ear. Did you undulate your sexy little body against him like you did me?" Jet knew he was being unduly cruel for saying such a thing. But he couldn't dam his raging jealousy. He was too frustrated.

Adele felt ill. *Was that what Jet thought of her? Did he think she would behave like that with another man?* She moaned. *No. I would never . . . ! could never . . .*

But it was too late. Jet lips claimed hers angrily. She had never imagined such a brutish kiss from him. She didn't want him to kiss her like that, in anger. Her hands pushed weakly against the wall of his chest. But as Jet's ravaging kiss continued, her traitorous body began to yield to him. Of their own volition her arms went about him. She gave a soft cry of surrender and let him have his way with her mouth. Then the urgent savagery of Jet's kiss evolved into urgent tenderness. Adele didn't want him to ever stop. And his gentle onslaught continued, until Adele wished that she could melt into his very soul.

Jet looked down on Adele's lovely upturned face and he knew that she was his for the taking. Possess her he would. Not now. Adele had a lot of growing up to do. To make love to her at this juncture was taboo. Adele didn't even know her own worth and uniqueness. He would have to wait until Adele grew out ofliving her life vagariously through the characters of the multitude of books she had read and old movies she watched religiously.

Jet couldn't pry his eyes away from Adele's beautiful upturned face. He was so tempted to kiss her some more. He dared not because he would not be able to stop.

"Lately, Adele you have done your darndest to seduce me, manipulate me into making love to you. I tell you, I see through your little game to make me jealous. At first I didn't but I do now." The way you looked at me when you came into the ball tonight, I knew it was all just a game."

"How childish can you get Adele? Did you really think your little antics would make me jealous enough to throw caution to the wind and make love to you?"

Adele felt shamed to the marrow.

Jet raged. "In the past, your antics have amused me. But this little game sure in hell didn't.'

Adele was mortified, bewildered. Things weren't going as she'd planned. With every once of strength she could muster, considering the circumstances, she tried to pull away from Jet. But she couldn't. His hold on her was stronger than saddle leather. Jet eyes were feverish. Despite his words, Adele knew that he wanted her.

As if he had read her thoughts, he barked, I'll be damned ifl allow your little game to force me into doing something that I feel is unwise." Adele hear me good and for once in your life take heed, I will not tolerate such games. "You, belong to me," he told her, his voice gruff with suppressed passion. "And don't you ever forget that it is to me that you belong." Adele I want you to know that in the future I will not tolerate such foolish games as the outrageous game you played this evening.

The memory of the sweetness of her delectable little body made Jet ache to take her then and there and it angered him because he knew he shouldn't. "You're mine Adele, every inch of you," he reinerated his voice a possessive caress.

This time he thundered down into her upturned face, "And I will not tolerate a repeat of this evening's spectacle."

She had thought she would die when Paulette had shown her Jet's marriage proposal note." Jet might own her heart, but he didn't own her. She would not be his plaything.

Adele tore herself from Jet's embrace. Still heaving, she told him in a voice that was raw from suppressed pain and anger. "Jet the mansions, the horses, the cars, the airplanes, the yachts and your damnable millions all belong to you. But I don't.' And with all the dignity she could muster, she told him. "Jet if you will excuse me, I'm going to find my date and have him take me home." Then Adele ran from the room not caring that she almost knocked Mignon Trideaux down in her haste to get away from Jet.

Jet set down unsteadily on the side of his desk. He raked his hands through his thick hair. What the hell was he going to do with his little spitfire? Adele with her beguiling games of late could in an instant plummeted him to a hell of agonizing jealousy and in the next instant melt in his arms and make him soar to the heavens. What was he going to do with Adele? He was going to marry her, if her love for him was geniune and not just a fantasy she was caught up in for the moment.

"What's done in the dark will come to the light."

"Mother how long how have you been lurking about in my doorway and what in the world do you mean by that remark?" I've made no secret of how I feel about Adele."

"But you've kept it in the dark about who she is." "What?"

"Stop pretending Jet. I know. Did you think I wouldn't investigate the little golddigger's background?" I had her family tree traced back a hundred years or more. The detective I hired faxed me a full report shortly before the ball." I know exactly who she is."

"Well you know more than I do. Jet reply. you hurt your mother in this way?" The evidence is right here in black and white."

For the first time' Jet noticed the white paper that was a stark contrast to the glittering black gown that his mother was wearing.

"Dear God, Jet. How could you get involved with the niece of your father's mistress?" I thought you had more decency than that." I always suspected that girl was trash. Now I know."

Jet felt as if he had been kicked in the stomach by one of his large throughbreds.

"Good Gracious, Lord. Jet you are as white as a sheet. You really didn't know." I wonder if this isn't worse than you having known. Obviously, you became involved with this girl without checking out her background. A man in your position should never do such a foolhardy thing." Mignon's eyes glittered with triumph. "Now that you know, I know you will do the right thing and end this relationship before it goes any further."

"And what ifi don't?"

"You can't be considering for a second to maintain a relationship with this woman knowing the pain it would cause your mother." I know you care more about my feelings and happiness than that."

Chapter Eleven

Adele found Jonny and they said good night to his parents, and they Adele, what happened?" You look stricken." Jonny turned to Adele the moment they were seated in his car.

"It didn't work Jonny." She sobbed. She took the white handkerchief that Jonny offered her. She dabbed at her streaming eyes, in total disregard to her make-up. "Jet's never going to truly love me." He's already asked Paulette to marry him. "I'm just some silly Iii toy, he thinks he owns."

"You're mistaken Adele. Jet cares a lot about you. Besides Jet's a pretty decent person. Jonny's half-hearted comforting probably sounded ineffectual even to him.

"I'm not mistaken, Jonny. Jet told me that I belonged to him." "I'm afraid that his claim is true. She wailed softly. "I do belong to him because I love him more than anything on earth. I've been deluding myself. I realize that now. She added between sobs. "Oh Jonny, please take me home. "I just want to go home."

"Adele I can't take you home this upset. What will your parents think?"

"They will think that I had a miserable time and start asking a lot of questions.

"Then we need to get you calmed down and repair your makeup."

Jonny pointed out sensibly

"Only a little bit. Once we get the mascara wiped off you won't look like a raccoon anymore." Jonny teased. "Have you eaten anything?"

"Not a bite." I prepared most of the hors-d'oeuvres for the ball and didn't eat a single one."

"For a man whose suppose to be so smart, Jet is sure making a big mistake letting you get away. "It's not often you find a woman who looks like you and can cook too!" Hell I would marry you myself ifI was the marrying kind." He laughed.

Adele had to smile inspite of her unhappiness. "Jonny, I've only known you for a short while but you're a very good friend."

"And you are a good friend to me to Adele. I knew right off that I could trust you. "Heck you already know where all my skeletons are." He laughed once more. "Is there a hamburger joint open around here. "I'm ravished. I have eaten a thing either."

Adele and Jonny had driven to the next town to a late night hamburger place and eaten. It was well after mid-night when Jonny had brought her home. Adele had reapplied her makeup and Jonny had managed to make her laugh a lot. She was in much better spirits. Her mother and daddy didn't suspect a thing. She described to her parents how the ballroom had looked and she told them about Wynton's playing and named all the important people that she saw. Not once did she let on that the ball had turned out to be the worse night of her life.

Marie—142

Adele awakened the next morning to the sound of vigorous activity. "What's going on in here?" She asked. The living room was crowded with suit cases and coolers and such.

"Don't you remember? We leave for Atlanta this morning."

For the last few days, Adele had been so occupied with the ball and everything she had totally forgotten that her parents would be going on their first real vacation, ever.

"C'mon sleeping beauty, help me get some ofthis stuff in the R.V." Her daddy ordered playfully as he came through the door.

"Wrong fairytale, Zach." Her mother chuckled. She picked up a small suitcase. "Adele is our little Cinderella."

"To bad, the Prince doesn't think so." Adele anquished in silence. Fifteen minutes later, they had loaded the last of the stuff. Adele gave her parents a dutiful good bye kiss. She disembarked. And she stood back to wave goodbye.

"You behave yourself, while we are gone Adele. Her daddy yelled from the window as he pulled off. God, if only she had behaved the night before.

"The memory ofthe ball, Paulette's revelation, and Jet's anger crushed down on her with the force of a hundred stampeding horses. She wanted to crawl back in her bed and never get out again. Jet was engaged. Jet was engaged. For the first time since Jet had came into her life, she didn't have a solution. She didn't have a plan. It was Sunday. She decided she would go back to bed, maybe she would fall into a pleasant dream, a dream where she and Jet were together forever.

When Adele arrived at Jet's on Monday morning, Mignon Trideaux's numerous bags were being packed into her Black Mercedes by a ranch hand. "A few days before, Adele would have found pleasure in Mignon's departure. But it didn't matter anymore. She didn't stand a chance with Jet, now. The only thing that Adele hoped for was that she didn't run into Paulette. She most likely had spent the rest of the weekend with Jet.

"There's not much for you to do here today. Mignon told Adele coldly. Her descent down the stairs was deliberate and purposed. The caterers cleaned everything up. And if you expected to see Jet, he and Paulette were gone before I got out of bed this morning." "And I don't know when Jet will return.

Adele's heart sank further. She recognized in Mignon Trideaux's eyes triumph and pure hatred. She wondered what she had done to make the woman dispise her so much. Was been poor such a dispicable thing?

After Mignon had gone, Adele decided her first order of business would be to make the beds upstairs. Adele didn't delude herself about why she was so anxious to make the beds. She wanted to see just how many beds had been used over the weekend. She wanted to know whether Jet and Paulette had shared a bed. She was weak with relief to discovered that from all appearances Jet and Paulette had not shared the same bed. She hurriedly did Mignon's and Paulette's bed, but when she came to Jet's she lingered. Like some silly school girl, she dived into his bed and wrapped herself in his sheets. She luxuriated in the faint smell of Jet—his cologne, his soap, his essence.

As she lay there wrapped in Jet's sheets, the memory of how Jet had danced with her in New Orleans and his subsequent lovemaking afterward, filled Adele with an aching longing for Jet to finish what he had started.

She started daydreaming about what it would be like to belong to Jet totally. She drifted off to sleep.

It was mid-afternoon when Adele awakened from her nap in Jet's bed.

She quickly changed the sheets on Jet's bed. After she had finished, she realized that she was famished. She went down to the kitchen. There were a good many left over baked stuffed shrimp and baked stuffed crabs. She decided she would have that for her snack before she called it a day and went home. The ideal of going back to her house just to be alone didn't seem too appealing. She decided she might spend the night at Jet's. He wouldn't mind. Jet had a theatre room in his house and he was hooked up to cable. She would probably order in a movie or two. She was going to stuff herself on leftovers, watch a movie and get drunk on some of Jet's finest white wine. It had been one hell of a week and it was just one of those days. Besides, it was a good plan.

Adele went down to the wine cellar for the wine. She soon found the perfect wine, a 1980 Bordeaux. Since that was the year she was born it had to be a good year. But when she tried the door to leave, it wouldn't open. The doorknob would tum, but the door wouldn't bulge. God, Jet had mentioned that sometimes the door would get stuck due to some minor foundation problems he had to correct. Apparently some of the dirt he had used to build up the site was settling unevenly. Adele tried not to panic. open. It was to no avail. God, what a predictment in which she found herself. If only she had left the door ajar. She had no ideal when Jet would return, it could be days, even weeks. And no one knew she was in Jets house. Her parents wouldn't be back for another two weeks. And they probably wouldn't try to call her until another several days. And when they did, they probably wouldn't worry if they couldn't reach her. After all she had told them that she would be spending a great deal of time in Baton Rouge studying for finals in the university library. After ascertaining the direness of the situation, Adele did the only thing she could do at the time, she had a good cry.

After crying profusely for about fifteen minutes, Adele decided she would look for a telephone down there that she could use to call someone to come to the house and rescue her. A few minutes later she quailed that notion. There was no phone in the cellar. But she had discovered that there was a half bath, at least she could relieve herself if the need arose. And she would be able to wash up.

Adele found a corkscrew hanging on the wall. She opened the bottle of wine and took a large swig then slowly slid down the wall and settled down onto the floor. As she pondered her situation, a long bronze colored nail—another left over from the ball— traced the intricate pattern of the ceramic tile flooring of the cellar. Jet was off somewheres galavanting with Paulette, and might be days even weeks before he returned. Well, water was available. She could drink wine for nourishment, and there was a good venting system in the cellar that provided plenty air. Therefore, there was a pretty good chance she would not perish before she was found. That thought in mind she let herself drift off to sleep.

Something had awakened her. A sound. She shook her head to shake off the drowsiness. She listened. Then she heard another sound.

Movement. Someone was in the house. She scrambled off the floor as fast as she could. She made it up the short flight of stairs quicker than she had thought possible. She was ready to yell for help. But she had a frightening thought. The alarm system was off. What if there were burgulars in the house?

"Adele!"

It was Jet. Jet was home. Adele heaved a sigh of relief. "I'm down here Jet, in the wine cellar. She yelled as loud as she could. Jet must have seen her things upstairs and figured rightly she still had to be in the house since the alarm system was still off.

Seconds later, Jet gave the door a hard heave turned the knob once more and it was opened. Adele didn't think. She threw herself against Jet. She was so relieved to see him.

"Oh, baby, its a good thing I decided to come home tonight. "How long had you been stuck down there?" Jet anquished.

"Hours. Adele sobbed. I didn't think you were coming back anytime soon. I imagined that when you did finally return, you would find me nothing but skin and bones, crazy and drunk. Adele babbled between sobs and buried her face in Jet's chest. She luxuriated in the feel of his strong arms.

"Ssh." It's okay. I'm here. I'm here. Jet soothed. He began to kiss Adele tears away. Then his lips found hers.

A little voice in Adele's head was telling her that she should drag herself out of Jet's embrace because he was an engaged man. But she didn't want to listen. She did not listen. Jet's kiss was sweet and intoxicating. As the kiss deepened, Adele greedily drank its nectar. Her blood raced through her body and she was beginning to feel an out of body sensation of floating that was akin to when she was riding, soaring on the back of one of the Arabian horses who was drinking the wind.

Then Jet picked her up in his arms and carried her up the narrow back staircase to his room. Once in the bedroom, they sort of tumbled onto his bed together. Then Jet was kissing Adele as if he never wanted to stop.

For a very long time they just kissed and rolled about on the bed. Without taking his lips from Adeles, Jet took off his coat.

Adele didn't know where it came from, but she found her fingers helping Jet undo the buttons on his shirt. She felt his hot bared flesh as the shirt slipped from his shoulders. With a frantic urgency her hands kneaded his bared shoulders then his upper arms. The muscles beneath her fingers grew taut. She ached to feel more of him. Her hands traced an unsure little trail across the taut sinews of his chest. She dragged the heel of her hands across his swollen nipples then downward to the flat plains of his stomach. As her hands travelled lower, her questing fingers caused a deep shudder to rent him.

With a touch light as the cool air of the room, Adele traced his aroused manhood through the fabric of his slacks. A shudder stronger than the first one rent him.

Adele's sweet unsure touch caused the ground to shake beneath Jet. It rocked his world. He wanted her just that bad. But he wanted to be sure it was what she wanted too. Jet brought Adeles hands up to his lips and kiss first one then the other. Then his eyes probed deeply into hers.

"Is this what you want?" He queried softly.

"Yes." Adele answered. Just promise me you won't stop.

"I won't." He replied firmly. He couldn't stop even though he knew he should. Could he marry her now, knowing what he knew about her family history? Could marry her knowing that she would be plagued by his mother's animosity" But he couldn't contemplate the problems when his heart was pounding like the thundering hooves of race horses coming into the home stretch.

Jet pulled her upward until they were facing each other on their knees. He unloosened her thick hair from its ponytail and let it flow about her shoulders. One then the other, he slipped the straps of her overalls off her shoulders. Then he pulled her tee shirt over her head. In a few seconds, he dispensed with her bra and she was completely bared to the waist.

The cool air ofthe room blew tantalizing little kisses over Adele's swollen breast. A shudder of excitment rent her.

Jet slowly dipped his head until finally his lips claimed hers in a kiss as tender as the moonlight that flowed threw the sheer lace panels of the massive bedroom window. Adele melted into him. He groaned and lowered her to the bed then his lips traced a familiar route to her aching breast. While he kissed and suckled one breast he gently kneaded the other.

Adele arched deeply to meet his lips. Adele didn't even try to hold back the love cries that rose in her throat.

Similar to the way the pungent fragance of a bouquet of gradenias premeates a room, Adele's earthy cries of pleasure filled the room.

Jet couldn't get enough of the taste of Adele's sweet flesh. He quickly disposed of the rest of his clothing. Then he used his hands and mouth to rid her of the rest of her clothing. He kissed and licked the heated flesh on her legs, and thighs until her flesh quivered like tree moss caught in a spring breeze. He kissed upward to the point where her thighs joined. Then he tasted her secret delights. Adele's fingers were entwined in his hair and the heel of her hands applied a slow rhythmic pressure against his head that urged him closer. The sweet clean taste of her made him want to positively devour her. But his loving cup threatened to runneth over and he dared not linger. Instead, he dragged his mouth away and continued an upward path over her quivering flesh. Once again, he captured a turgid nipple. His tongue did a slow undulating dance with it.

"Jet, please." Adele cried.

Jet positioned himself above her and looked into her beautiful eyes, questioning. He wanted to be sure without a doubt this was what she wanted.

"Adele, are you sure this is what you want

"Oh Jet, please don't stop. You promised you wouldn't." Adele cried. Jet slowly dipped his head until his lips touched hers. At first his lips glazed with the taste of her body splash and the essence of her flesh glided across Adeles lips in a glib waltz. Adele wanted more, she surrendered her mouth to him and their tongues met, embraced and did an undulating slow drag of a dance together. Their nude heated bodies emulated their entwined tongues and began to wither and undulated one against the other. Every time Jet's aroused manhood touched her body a soft little moan would escape Adele's throat only to meet Jet's answering moan.

Their kisses became frantic. Jet was kissing her face, her ears, her throat. And her mouth and tongue were tasting his face, and his throat.

Adele couldn't get enough of the taste of him or the feel of his taut body undulating against hers. No matter how much she pressed her body against Jet's or how tightly she held him, it was not enough. She wanted more. She ached to be closer. She wanted to be one with him. "Jet, I ache so." She cried. Then Adele took Jet's hand and pressed it against her lower stomach and showed him where the ache was. "Please make it stop." She begged.

"Adele, baby do you know what you are doing to me?" Jet cried.

Adele trembled as Jet parted her legs and lowered himself into position.

Jet hesitated for a moment. Mon Dieu. He didn't want to hurt her. He knew it was best to make it as quick as possible. He thrusted hard enough to break through the barrier. Adele's soft yep of pain was almost his undoing. He gently cradled her to him as if she was as fragile as a bird. He gave her slow and wet kisses until he could feel her relax against him. And then and only then did he start to move inside of her. Then she was moving with him. And the hot velvety sheaths of her womanhood closed about him, nibbling at him, holding him in sweet agonizing ecstasy. Jet emitted primitive cries such that he had never uttered before.

Adele cries of pleasure were just as intense as Jet's. She had not known. She had not imagined that such ecstasy was possible. It was a miracle. It was a wonder. It was beautiful. This was her moment with Jet. The moment that would have to last a lifetime. The love she felt for Jet manifested itself in the way she gave herself to him. She didn't hold back, anything. She wantonly pushed her body up to meet his devastating thrusts time after time. As they moved together in perfect harmony, Adele could no longer distinguish where she began and where Jet ended. She was melting into his body, into his soul. The sensation of mind out ofbody intensified. She was floating with him, suspended in midair and time. "Open your eyes, Adele, Jet commanded. I want you to see how you make me feel," he s id. His voice was hoarswith passion.

Adele obeyed. She could not deny him, anything. So she looked at him, as he strained above her. His black eyes were feverish with p ssion, and a thin veil of perspiration covered qis entire body. All ofher dreams and all of her fanatasies had not prepared her for the beauty she found in Jet's eyes. "It's so beautiful, I can't bear it," Adele cried. And she could not bear it. Something was happening. Her body tighten about Jet and pulled him to the very core of her womanhood. Once again she felt the out of body sensation of floating, being suspended in midair as her body rode powerful spasmodic slivers of pleasure. Adele wrapped her arms and thighs around Jet's back tighter and held on for dear life as she rode toward ecstasy.

Unparalleled pleasure. Unparalleled pleasure was what Jet felt as Adele's womb enfolded him in a spastic embrace. He had wanted more than anything to give her pleasure. He had wanted her first time to be special. And he had succeeded. It had taken a superhuman effort for him to hold back the release that his three years of celibacy demanded. From the first day that he had met Adele he had known that he loved her, and he had not desired any other woman since. How could he, when thoughts of her had dominated his awake hours and haunted him in his dreams? His heart had reasoned that he would've been untrue to the love he felt, if he had slept with another woman. The years he'd waited had tortured him. At last it was over. He gave in to the ecstasy that rocked **him.** "Adele!" He cried and collapsed against her.

After the loving, Adele curled up **in** Jet's arms and fell asleep.

Chapter Twelve

It was morning. The golden glow of the morning sun filled the large bedroom. She was in bed with Jet! The memory of the ecstasy she had experienced in Jet's arms descended about her like a heavy cloak. She had let Jet make love to her, though he was engaged to another woman. She had thought she was a better person than that. She studied the man who was still fast asleep. He needed a shave. Irregardless of her feelings of guilt, a thrilled of pleasure streaked through Adele. She had often imagined what he would look like in the morning. Now she knew. Despite the black stubble on his face, he looked younger. His features were uncharacteristically relaxed. Adele had not thought it possible to love Jet anymore than she already loved him. But she had been wrong. Now that she knew him totally, her loved for him had multiplied, intensified. And it would continue to grow. As she watched him sleep, the memory of the beauty she had seen in his eyes when he loved her was a tantalizing caress. A caress that she could easily become addicted to pretty much like the addict to drugs and the gambler to high risk. She knew that in the future, even when he was married to Paulette, anytime that Jet wanted her she wouldn't be able to deny him.

To be the other woman was unbearable. She would not become that in Jet's life. She was going to end it now. And she knew how. Had he not at every interval took pains to determined it was what she wanted also.

Jet's sense of honor and pride would never let him approach her again when she was finished. She had to convince him that it hadn't been what she wanted after all.

Adele eased out of the bed, and creeped over to the dresser. She found a pen and pad. She quietly picked up her scattered clothing. Then she went into the bathroom and sat on the floor on a plush throw rug. Still nude, she wrote Jet a short letter. Basically, she stated that it had been a mistake. She regretted giving herself to him. She wrote that she was quitting her job because she didn't ever want to see him again. When she was finished writing, the blue notepaper was stained with her tears. She put on her clothes, tipped back into the bedroom and lay her note on the pillow beside Jet. As Adele left the bedroom, she felt as if she was the walking dead. She was numb with pain. But it was best to severe her ties with Jet now, than to suffer the slow agonizing death of being his mistress.

The golden glare of the sun awakened Jet. It had to be late morning. When had he last, if ever, slept so long and soundly. *Adele.* He turned over to kiss his baby good morning. He found a note instead. He read the tear stained note at least ten times, trying to make sense of it. Had he imagined Adele's pleasure. No. It didn't make sense. Unless Adele realized after it was over that she really didn't love him. And it was only a fantasy that she had lived out and was ready to put it behind her. Now, she was filled with regret because she realized the precious thing she had given him— her virginity—she could never get it back. *Mon Dieu. What have I done?* Jet lamented silently. Had he in his love and his uncontrollable need to possess her, seduced a young woman who was simply living out one of her fantasies. He had known that Adele spent a lot of time fantasizing about life. Yet, he had allowed himself to be mislead by her beguiling little games. With his experienced kisses and caresses, it had been easy for him to convince Adele that she wanted him as much as he wanted her. God, he had overpowered her. He had done the unforgivable. His first thought was to seek Adele and beg her forgiveness. How could he ask Adele to forgive him when he'ld never be able to forgive himself? Besides what did he have to offer her anyway? A few stolen moments here and there. If he marrried Adele, his mother would make her life a living hell.

If it hadn't been for Jonny, Adele would have probably lost her mind.

Or worst, she would have gone flying back into Jet's arms. But Lonny proved to be a rock. In the evenings he would come out to visit Adele and bring funny old movies for them to watch. It was a blessing that he was with Adele the evening that Jet in a news conference announced that

Sanfroid would be entered in the Kentucky Derby that May. The news conference was aired live from Fiveforks on CNN. The Fiveforks team was present with Jet, Mr. Thiboudeaux, Anthony, Dr. Jose Rodriguez, the breeder and of course Sangfroid. "I should have been there too." Adele had sobbed on Lonny's shoulder. "Jet, didn't even bother to let me know that he was calling a news conference. Adele was besides herself

"What you expect, Adele?" "Didn't you write that you never wanted to see Jet again?" Jonny reminded her, patiently. Then he just sat quietly while she cried her heart out. When she was finished he put on some silly old movie. With Jonny, Adele didn't have to put up a front like she did at the university. In the past few days, Adele had just gone through the motions of attending her classes. Half the time, she had no idea what was gomg on. A few evenings later, Adele made an half-hearted attempt to study for her finals. She realized that if she let her grades slip she would lose her scholarship. She gave herself a strict talking to and started studying as best she could which wasn't laudable. Then she did what she had always done when she was lonely or miserable, she put on some Mozart and lost herself in the music. Soon she was able to concentrate. She was studying seriously when the phone rang. Adele reluctantly turned down the stero system and dragged herself to the phone. She knew it would be her mother even before she hard the familiar cheerful greeting.

"Hi, baby. "I'm surprised Jonny didn't answer the phone." Lorraine Baychan teased her daughter.

"Jonny's not here tonight, I'm studying for finals. Adele explained. It had been so hard talking to her mama each night and pretending everything was just fine. But this phone call seemed a little easier. Mozart was working his magic. In addition, her mother seemed more excited and cheerful than usual.

"Adele, everybody your father and I have talked to today here in Atlanta want to talk about one thing and one thing only. Her mothers words tumbled over each other. Sangfroid and the Kentucky Derby is all the rage up here." "Everybody is saying that he most likely will win. Your daddy and me are almost celebrities because we come from St. Pierre, Louisiana.

Can you believe that, baby? Who would have ever thought such a thing that lil old St. Pierre would be on everybody's lips?"

But before Adele could answer, her mother rushed on. Everybody is saying that if Sangfroid wins, Jet will be the first African-American who owned a horse that won the Kentucky Derby."

Adele ignored the fist of pain that closed about her heart at the mere mentioning of Jet's name. "That's not true Mama." I am afraid that Jet will be the second African-American whose horse won the Derby. A black man named Dudley Allen won it in 1891."

Lorraine Baychan chuckled. "Only a history genius like you Adele would know something like that." She pointed out proudly. Anyway, most people don't know that and they are going wild about Jet here. I mean wild."

Her mother talked excitedly a few moments longer. Adele even said hello to her father. But everything she said or did, she seemed to do by rote in a thick mist. Her mother's call had caused her to lose her focus once more. God, what was happening to her? Why couldn't she seem to get it together? She had been so afraid that she would run into Jet at the ranch, she hadn't even bothered to visit Sangfroid in several days. Soon he would be leaving for Louisville. The first Saturday in May when the Kentucky Derby was held was only two weeks away. She had to see Sangfroid before he was shipped off. But she was so afraid what might happen if she ran into Jet. Not a night had passed that she had not dreamed of him, reliving their lovemaking. The dreams were so vivid and real she actually screamed out his name. But could she risk seeing Jet? She never wanted Jet to know that most of what she had written in that damnable note was a big fat lie. She could never truly regret giving herself to him. She just regretted that he was engaged to another woman.

Before Adele crawled into bed that night she made a call to Jonny. She had asked him to accompany her to the ranch to see Sangfroid. She needed him for moral support in case she ran into Jet.

"Adele, this place is tighter than Fort Knox. Lonny complained.

They had just gone through the third security check point and they were yet to reach the stables. "Sangfroid has become national known and very important." Jet's not taking any chances that he might be horseknapped or worst harmed by some fanatic or enemy of his. Adele explained. Though she understood Jet's motivation for such strict security, still it felt strange to see security guards packing high powered rifles. Fiveforks had changed overnight. It didn't seem like the same place in which she had frolicked for the past three years. But then she had also changed overnight. She had gone from an inexperienced girl who had believed in happy ever after endings to love stories to an experienced woman who didn't know how she was going to bear not having Jet in her life.

Jet was in the stables making sure everything had been done that should be done so that Sangfroid's departure the that day to Louisville would go without mishap. He sensed Adele's presence the moment she entered the stables. He had known she would come. There was no way she would let Sangfroid leave without her seeing him. She loved that horse too much. He just wish she loved him half as much. She didn't ever want to see him again. And it was eating at him. It was killing him. For the past few days he had barely eaten or slept.

"Doc Zanders, this is Jonathan Adams, Jr. Adele introduced Jonny to Jet's horse breeder.

Adele sweet voice forced Jet to look in her direction even though he didn't want to. And when he did, jealousy wrapped in heartache made him clench his jaws. Adams was hovering about her like a protective horse blanket.

"And this tall dark and handsome fellow over here is my baby. This is Sangfroid." Jet heard Adele tell Adams." Jet wished that he could introduce her to the whole world as his baby, his heart. But he couldn't. Adele didn't want to be with him. And all he could do was hide behind his dark glasses and stare at her. She didn't look as if she was any happier than he. The dark shadows beneath her eyes were a give away that she had not been sleeping well. She probably had been crying a lot too. It was all his fault. He had done this to her. The last thing on earth he had wanted to do was hurt Adele. But he had, anyway. He had seduced her and she was miserable because she was in love with another man not him.

"It can't be done." That's what well meaning friends and business advisors had told him when he had shown them the plans for Fiveforks. With an image of Adele always far most in his mind he had moded and shaped a veritable swamp land into a beautiful and thriving horse ranch. For most of his life, if he wanted to do something, he simply did it. He had wanted Adele more than he had ever wanted anything. So he had made her his and he had probably destroyed her in the process. Jet was finding it unbearable to gaze upon what his selfishness had wrought.

"Is he gone, Jonny?"

"He's gone Adele.

Adele didn't know whether to be relieved or breakdown and cry. Jet had not spoken to her and she had not spoken to him. Were they the same two people who had argued and teased each other for hours sometimes? It was hard to believe that their relationship had deteriorated to such an extent. But it was the only way. At that very moment, it was all she could do to keep from seeking him out. She had this urge to see if he was all right. The dark glasses he wore had not concealed that he was not looking his best. And his clothes had fit him a bit loosely. She wondered if he was eating right. God, had he forgotton how to use a shaving razor? Jet looked as miserable as she felt. Instinctly, she knew that she was probably the cause for Jet's unhappiness. He was feeling guilty. She wanted to go to him and relieve him of that guilt. But that was not feasible. As long as Jet was feeling guilty, then he would stay away from her. She needed him to stay the hell away from her. Because if he so much as touched his fingertip to any part of her, she would be in his arms in an instant.

Adele knew she couldn't stay in for very long. Jet could return at any moment. She took a long final look at the horse that was dear to her. She caressed the fine silky hair of Sangfroid's broad forehead. His large horse eyes that often surveyed life from a dispassionate point of view seemed to warm to her in their usual way. "When you race at the Derby do what comes natural for you. Drink the wind." "Just drink the wind like you always do." She reminded him. "Bonheur." Then she gave Sangfroid a kiss on his forhead for good luck.

"Adele! Girl aren't you a sight for sore eyes. Where you been keeping yourself?' Eddie Thiboudeaux had spotted Adele and was heading toward her.

"Let's go now, Jonny." Adele demanded softly. She pulled at Jonny's arm.

Jonny was hesitant. "What's going on? Jet's gone.

"I just can't bear to talk with Mr. Thibodeaux right now. Adele tried to explain. Adele's eyes welled with tears.

The sight of Adele tears spurred Jonny to action. He hurriedly got her out of the stables and to his car.

After Adele and Jonny's abrupt departure, Eddie went in search of an explanation. He found Jet in the tack room above the stables. He studied Jet's rigid profile for a moment. Eddie wondered how it was possible that a man who had the world at his feet could possibly look as unhappy as Jet Trideaux did.

"Jet what the dickens is going on around here?" Adele just flew out of the stables like a stampede of mad horses were chasing her." "Jet, that girl is as much a part of Sangfroid's team as you, Doc Zanders, Anthony and me, maybe moreso.

Eddie's awkward use of the acronym instead of his usual reverent Mr. Trideaux caused Jet's lips to pucker into an odd little smile that didn't reach his eyes. His fingers closed about the supply ledger that he was holding in a vise grip similar to the knot in his gut. He didn't want to discuss Adele with anyone, not even Eddie.

"Eddie what makes you think I know what is going on with Adele?" She has a life beyond Fiveforks, you know."

Eddie was taken back by the amount of bitterness he detected in Jet's tone.

"What I do know is that whatever is going on with that little gal is going on with you, also. Eddies eyes trained in on Jet. "Both ofya look as unhappy as two scalded cats.

Jet didn't look up from the ledger in his hand. He mumbled offhandedly, "Everything seemed to be in order."

"Order!" Eddie barked. "From the looks ofya, order is the last thing you have in your life. "Hell man you're reading with shades on. Or have you even noticed? "You've messed up things with Adele haven't, you?

Jet visibly flinched. "Eddie you've said enough." Jet intoned coldy.

"No, I haven't. I'm just getting started. Sure of his place in Jet's life,

Eddie continued. He had given Jet fatherly advise before and Jet had usually taken it.

"I knew you was making trouble for yourself, when I spotted that Paulette Joseph here not to long ago." The recollection made Eddie feel weary and he plopped down onto the nearby leather loveseat.

"Whatever the problem is, that woman is at the root of it."

Jet snapped the ledger he was holding shut and looked at Eddie for the first time since he had entered the room. Jet took off his dark glasses and look Eddie straight in the eyes and said. "Paulette has nothing to do with the mess I've made with Adele. I'm the one totally responsible." "I should have taken your advise Eddie."

The pain Jet was feeling he had not tried to conceal from Eddie. Eddie was the nearest thing he had to a father since he had lost his father when he was barely fifteen. He wished that he could tell Eddie about what had happened between Adele and him, but it was too private. He couldn't discuss that even with Eddie. Instead he said. "Eddie it's about time we get the caravan on the road. "It time you all head out for Louisville."

Eddie stared at Jet for a long moment as if he wanted to say something but thought better of it. Then he said. "Sanfroid is being loaded up in the trailer as we speak."

"Well, I see you all in a few days in Louisville."

"Aren't you coming with us?"

No. I'll be leaving for Hawaii in a little while.

CHAPTER THIRTEEN

It was late afternoon. Jonny had just left. He had promised that he would call Adele later that evening. Adele was lying on the couch crouching on pop com and watching a soap opera when she heard the roar. She ran to a window and looked out. It was Jet's latest and most expensive toy—his bizjet as he called it. It was just getting airborn and it was close. Adele felt that if she got up on their roof she would be able to jump up and touch its sleek black body. Adele found herself going out onto the porch of their double-wide then into the yard to watch the magnificent aircraft climb heavenward. A river of proud in Jet and all that he had accomplished flowed through her. She bet she wasn't the only local watching Jacques Trideaux take off. James, Jet's pilot had grown up in St. Pierre and his parents and everyone else in St. Pierre were proud of him. When James had landed the big jet plane for the first time in St. Pierre a few weeks earlier a lot of people including Adele had gone out to see him do it.

For sure, she had gone to the airport to watch a homeboy land a big private jet, but most of all she had gone to see Jet return home after being away for over a month. The airfield had been crowded with people. It had to be at least a couple of hundred people present. Adults and small children shield their eyes with their hands from the bright glare of the mid-morning sun as their eyes trained the sky for a glimpse of the plane. Then someone who'd had the foresight to bring binoculars had spotted the jet as it came in from the east.

Adele's heart had almost stopped beating as she watched the large jet speed down the runway that didn't look as if it was long enough. At the end ofthe runway was the impending swamp. But James had brought the plane to a complete stop about three-hundred feet short of the end of the runway.

"What a landing!" The crowd had yelled, whistled and hooted uproariously. It was hard to determined who they were most proud of, James for such a spectacular landing or Jet for owning such a spectacular piece of machinery. Adele would remember for all eteminty how she had felt at the sight of Jet exiting the plane. He had looked tired but elated. His eyes had frantically searched the crowd until they had landed on her. He had given her a pert wave and she had waved back. And for the first time, she had known by the way her skin tingled and the tantalizing ache in her private parts that she wanted to make love with Jet more than anything.

Adele had not rushed out onto the runway to greet the two heroes. Instead she had remained in her well chosen spot atop her dad's pickup truck and watched all the excitment. James and Jet had patiently given the kids a tour of the jet. They were both such good role models for the local youths.

Now, as the jet turned westward Adele sighed deeply. She felt a little anxious for Jet's safety. James was an excellent pilot she knew. Hadn't she heard Jet bragged about how he had managed to land the jet on a gravel runway in a rain storm somewhere in Latin America and hadn't so much as put a tiny dent on the plane. But she worried about Jet anyway. She who had flown only once in her entire life was not yet comfortable with the thought of just jumping onto a plane and flying off to whereever. She could bear Jet being married to another woman. But she would not be able to bear it, if anything ever happened to Jet. "Dear God, please take care of him." She prayed out loud. Then she watched the plane until it was just a tiny black speck in the westward sky. *Godspeed Jet. Godspeed my love.*

She heard the phone ringing and she ran to answer it. It was probably her parents telling her that they had started out for home.

"I would like to speak to Tremaine Randall."

Adele paused for a moment at the use of her writing pseudonym. No one used that name but her agent. "This is she."

"Will you hold Ms. Randall, while I put Dotty Blake on the line." Adele slumped down in a seat. She wonder what was wrong. In all the commotion of the ball and Jet and her making love, she had totally forgotten that her historical romance book *Jass* had hit the bookstores earlier that week.

"Hi, Tremaine, Dotty here. "I just wanted to give my most profitable client a holler. "Are you seated my writing genius?" If not, you better pull up a chair. Dotty let go of one of her down home laughs.

"You know that your publisher initally agreed to a printing of fifty-thousand which was more than thirty thousand over the usual because he thought you had written a great book. 'Well let me tell you, Adele."

"Are you seated?

"I'm seated." Adele anwered drily. She was getting just a little bit tired of Dotty's theatrics.

Your *Jass* sold out its first fifty-thousand copies in a few days. "And as we speak, Notions books are printing up another two hundred thousand copies of your book. "It's a runaway bestseller babe."

Adele was glad that she was sitting. She couldn't believe what she was hearing.

"Are you sure about this Dotty?"

"Couldn't be more sure of anything." Just got off the phone with Tyler Spears over at Notions Books a few minutes ago. He wants two things from you Adele. First, he wants you to come to New York to confer with a director friend of his about doing a screenplay for a movie version of the book and secondly he wants you to go on a national tour to promote the book.

"But I can't do that Dotty." If this book becomes a movie or ifl go on tour everyone will know what I look like and who I am."

"I am afraid that Notions Books own the right to do as they please with your book. All they have to do is make sure you keep receiving the royalties for every book sold. And that gives them every right to tum this book into a movie." They didn't have to give you a shot at writing the screenplay.

God, she had never imagined that her book would be such a success. All she had wanted to do was write a book that expressed the way she felt about Jet. It had been such a beautiful dream. But now it was threatening to become a nightmare of gigantic porportions.

"Dotty is there away that all of this can happen with out anyone knowing about me, the author."

"I don't see how."

Dotty's answer dashed Adele's hope before it was fully formed. "Oh, Dotty, once it becomes known that I've had written a sultry historical romance, I can kiss goodbye any hope of ever being considered a serious scholar of history." Adele lamented. "You know this."

"I don't know any such thing." You're selling yourself short. That book you wrote is well-written. If it was just another run of the mill historical romance it wouldn't be selling like hotcakes. You wrote about a very serious subject, love. Love is the the thing that makes the world go round. It is time you stood back and took pride in what you have accomplished in writing this book."

Adele wondered if there was anyone on earth who could out talk Dotty.

"That reminds me, I had to send them a photo of you for the book jacket. The publishers want the latest copies to have a picture of you along with the biography you furnished before. Since the fat has hit the fan so to speak. Adele you might as well fax your true biography to me to forward to your publisher."

"I'll fax it to you tomorrow." Adele said dully.

"Stop sounding as if, I just asked you to put your head on the chopping block or worse. Besides, I need that fax like five minutes ago."

After she had faxed an authenic version of her biography, Adele felt totally drained. She had always prided herself in her ability to solve problems. Where were her problem solving skills now. Everything was spiralling out of control.

Jet smiled as he felt the almost imperceptible jerk that the bizjet made when it touched ground at New Orleans International Airport. James was one hell of a pilot. And in recent days he had become an equally good friend to Jet. While in Hawaii when he wasn't in business conferences Jet had found himself at loose ends. The hole in his stomach was burning like fire but it was a gift. At least the tormenting pain in his stomach made him forget about his heartache.

One night he an James had stumbled into each in a nightclub and hung out together. Jet had always respected James as a pilot and as a staff member of his mentor program. The next step friendship had came easy.

Jet had found himself discussing things with James that he had never discuss with anyone.

Do you believe in destiny James, and that some people are destined not to find happiness in life?"

"No. That's nonsense. Some people choose to be unhappy or they don't have the courage to risk it all to find happiness." But I never took you to be the type who wasn't willing to do what was necessary.

"What if my happiness causes much unhappiness for someone that I love dearly?

James pondered Jet's last question for a moment. "Man you've got me there, seems like you are between a rock and a hard place. You've damned if you do and you are damned if you don't.

"Precisely." Jet studied the ice cubes in his glass of milk for a moment longer. "I don't think I can give her up."

"I assume you're talking about Adele." This is all about Adele isn't it? Jet nodded.

"I don't understand, how could your being with a sweet girl like Adele be a problem." "It's a long story."

I've got plenty of time. Shoot."

Jet slammed back the remainder of his milk and did a quick perusal of the almost empty barroom. I think my hotel suite will provide even more privacy for us to talk."

Jet told James of his father death in a chartered airplane crash and how his father's mistress had died in the crash too. And he talked of his love for Adele and how his mother positively hated Adele because she bore a great resemblance to her aunt his father's mistress, Nadine Turner.

James studied Jet for a long moment. "Man that's a serious problem you have. But it's not an insurmountable one. "You love Adele don't you?"

"So much, I can't imagine life without her."

"I can believe it. Man you look like hell." Jet you can't keep putting yourself through this hell. You love Adele and she loves you." me. She loves Jonny Adams."

James laughed then said, "That's much to do about nothing. Adele's not serious about that Cassanova."

"Yes, she is."

"How do you know?"

"She told me so." She told me in the worst possible way, in a note." "In the note, she said that I was something she had to get out of her system and after making love with me she'd realized that it was Jonny that she really loved." God, how could I have been so danm selfish." I knew it was wrong of me to make love to her, but I did it anyway.

Chapter Fourteen

Mignon Trideaux almost lost her invariable composure at the sight of her son. He was not his usual impeccably dressed self. He was sporting blue jeans, a faded red polo shirt and white sneaker shoes. On his head he wore a red baseball cap. He needed a shave and he had lost weight.

"Good, Gracious Jet." Look at your face. You need a shave." You look like you haven't shaved in a month.

"Actually, it has been twenty days, Mother. I decided to start wearing a beard and mustache." Jet explained cooly. When in reality he hadn't shaved lately because he had trouble looking at himself in the mirror. He hadn't shaved since he had made love to Adele.

Mignon wasn't buying it though. "That explains the beard, but when is the last time you had a good nights rest."

Jet didn't answer.

His mother eyed him wearily. "Jet your sudden lack of interest in your appearance and your obvious unhappiness wouldn't have anything to do with that little golddigger in which you are infatuated, would it?"

Jet took a deep breath and exhaled slowly. "Mother, she's not a golddigger And I love her."

"Love her?" Jet how could you?" The girl is all wrong for you. She's unsuitable."

"Why is she unsuitable, mother?" Because she's Nadine Turner's niece? Mother that's very unfair. We don't get to choose our parents."

Mignon Trideaux looked as if she was about to say something but though better of it. Something in her son's demeanor stilled her tongue.

"It's not Adele fault that she resembles her Aunt Nadine."

His mother blanched. "I can't bear for you to continually speak that woman's name in this house!" She hissed vehemently.

"Mother do you think, that if we never say her name, somehow it will changed things." If her name is never said again on this earth, it will not alter the fact that she and daddy died together. "Mother you can't keep hiding from the truth. We have to discuss this. And this is as good a time as any."

"You talk about truth." Well, heres the truth. "The fact is your little Adele is unsuitable for you because she's common, trailor trash. But more importantly, she's not Creole. "She too damn dark. And if you were to marry her and have children with her, it would sully the Creole purity in the Trideaux family tree.

It was ironic that his mother thought that Adele was to dark-skinned for him to marry when in reality Adele probably had more caucasian blood running through her veins than he. Adele father was white by all appearances. James had told Jet that he could have gone up North an passed for white like the rest of his siblings had done. Instead he chosen to marry the woman that he loved and stayed in St. Pierre. But Jet didn't tell his mother this. It probably wouldn't have made any difference anyway. She couldn't see pass Adele's dark coloring. "Mama, I don't care about any of that." All that doesn't matter. It is love that matters. Love matters Mama, love."

Mignon eyes glittered with something akin to madness. "Do you think you are the only Creole man ever to fall in love with the wrong woman." Your father wanted to marry Nadine, too. But his parents talked some sense into him. In the end, he did the right thing."

"No mother, in the end he died with the woman that he loved." "Mama, I can't live a lie like that."

"You can, and you will." It is better that Adele marry someone like Jonathan Adams, Jr. He doesn't have two-hundred years of family history to uphold."

"Well, Mama you're be getting your wish. Adele probably will marry Jonny Adams. But not because I decided that she wasn't good enough for me. But because she decided that I was not good enough for her."

What are you saying, Jet. "I'm saying that Adele doesn't love me.

"Because if she did, nothing on this earth would stop me from marrying her."

Don't you see that it is for the best, Jet honey?" Now, you can go ahead and marry Paulette.

No, mother. I will not marry Paulette. I don't love her. That would be too cruel."

"My dear son, you are so much like your father, though you try not to be like him. You hurt me too."

Something in Jet cracked. He put his arms around his mother. "Mama, I don't mean to cause you any more pain. I just want to be happy.

"You can be happy Jet, if you will just let yourself be. Paulette would make the perfect wife."

"But I don't want the perfect wife. I want Adele." Jet made an attempt to make the situation less intent.

"There was a time when you wanted Paulette. You were even considering marrying Paulette. She called me a few years back and said that you had asked her to marry you.

Jet laughed. He recalled the ridiculous proposal he had made on the back of one of his business cards of all things. It wasn't very romantic. He had been very drunk when he had made it. "But, you know Paulette didn't hold me to that proposal. She opted to wait for me to ask again when I was sober."

"And you would have asked Paulette again, if that conniving little slut, Adele, hadn't came into your life."

"Mother, Adele is not a slut. She is far from it." He knew that better than anyone. "I didn't ask Paulette again, because I realized that I didn't love her and that when I married I wanted more than just the perfect match.

A few days after his proposal to Paulette, he had met Adele. And known for the first time what it was like to fall in love.

"Paulette loves you Jet." And it would make me very happy if she was the mother of my grandchildren."

"Mama, I spent most of my life trying to make you happy, trying to make up for the pain Daddy caused you. But I can't sacrifice my entire life to pay a debt that I don't owe." Daddy who was weak and selfish owes that debt, Mama. Daddy not me."

Mignon's beautiful face crumbled. "My dear son, is that what I've done to you. I've made you shoulder the burden of your daddy's shortcomings."

"No, Mama, I'm the one who took on that burden. "I wanted to be the perfect son. I wanted to make up to you for what Daddy had done. "So I tried to better him at everything. Instead of the state university, I graduated from Harvard. I've made more money than he would have dreamed of making. There's so much we will never be able to spend it. Your grandchildren won't be able to spend it, Mama." But like Daddy, I made a mess of my life."

"What, are you talking about Jet."

"It's a long story. Suffice to say, I've lost Adele. And I just don't know what I'm going to do with the rest of my life."

"Good gracious, Jet. I'll tell you what you are going to do with the rest of your life. In two days, you've got a Derby to win. Right now that's all you need to concentrate on. You can sort your life out later." Jet might be miserable now but he would thank his lucky stars one day that he hadn't tied himself for life to that little heartbreaker Adele. They were staunch Catholics and didn't believe in divorce. Paulette was a much more suitable woman to share the rest of Jet's life.

Before Jet had reached the end of the walk-way, Mignon was on the phone talking to Paulette. She told Paulette where Jet would be staying in Louisville.

"Jet this Paulette." I was wondering if you would like some company tonight. "They don't call us the new jet set for nothing. I could hop on a Lear and be there in less than two hours. Maybe we could have a late dinner together or something." Paulette suggested.

Jet knew that his mother was behind the call. When would his mother stop trying to orchestrate a marriage between him and Paulette. Obviously, not a word of what he had told her had any impact. "I know that mother put you up to this call. "To be frank with you, Paulette, I'm in a lousy mood and I would probably be a terrible dinner companion." Jet told Paulette.

"Yes, your mother did call. She's very concerned about you. "I'm sorry that you are going through a rough time. You know I'm always going to think of you as a friend and hope you think the same of me. "Would it be okay ifi joined you at the Derby for moral support tomorrow?" Paulette asked.

"Jet hesitated a moment before answering. "Sure, if you don't mind my poor company." Mother decided not to come, and it would be nice to have an old friend in my comer rooting for my horse."

"Well, tomorrow it is. When and where should we meet?

"The Eclipse Room at eleven. The race is at noon." Jet told her. He wondered if it was a mistake. Was he being unfair to Paulette? Maybe she still had some hope that he would propose to her again one day. It wasn't going to happen. As long as he loved Adele the way that he did, he would not marry another woman. It would be too cruel.

"What in the world happened to you Jet?" Paulette exclaimed. "And you look lovely as usual, Paulette. Jet said. His voice was touched with humor.

"Jet I'm serious. You've lost weight and it doesn't look as if you slept in a week."

"I've been very busy." Jet forced lightness into his tone. Paulette are you going to stand there and gawk at me or are you going to join me for a drink or something on the dinning terrace. It's such a beautiful morning".

Undaunted Paulette said. You've always had a hectic business schedule, but it has never affected you like this." Mignon tried to prepare me, but dear Lord, Jet.

"I'll be fine Paulette. Jet said as he held Paulette's chair. "Just give me a little space here."

On that first Saturday in May, not a soul was stirring about in St. Pierre. It was high noon. Every able body was glued in front of a television set. They were looking at scenes of stately Churchill Downs. Many had gone to the local civic center to watch the Derby on the giant screen that had been set up for the momentous event. Most of the people in St. Pierre made their livelihood either at the cellulose plant or Fiveforks. It was only natural that they were concerned about what was happening in Louisville at that moment.

Adele like everyone else in St. Pierrre was watching the event. Her daddy, mother and she had decided to watch the Derby at home not the local civic center.

The program announcer allotted a great deal of coverage to Jacques Trideaux. A short biography of Jet was read. Charismatic they described him. Even though the odds were five to one against Sangfroid winning, the horse was generating a lot of excitment. The sentiment was that he would at least place or show. There was a record crowd in attendance and a record number of African Americans in attendance.

Adele was trying her best to concentrate on what was going on and what was being said. However, it was not easy. For the past several days, she had been suffering from lower stomach cramps—the kind that usually signalled the beginning of her cycle. Albeit, nothing had happend so far. After a week of cramping she was five days late. She had never been late. A person could set their watch by her cycle that was how regular and predictable she had always been. There was this nagging little voice at the back of her mind that kept trying to come to the forefront. It was unthinkable. She wouldn't let the thought surface.

"There's Mr. Trideaux." Her mother cried. The cameras were trained on Jet as he entered one of the private owners boxers. The sight of him even if it was on television made Adele's heart do its telltale oflove. It skipped a beat. Jet's new mustache and beard gave him a rugged look.

Sexy. Then Adele saw that he was not alone. He was accompanied by his fiancee Paulette Joseph. *Dear God, would the sight of them together ever not hurt so much.*

Adele gripped a throw pillow. It took all of her willpower not to bolt from the room.

"They're off!" Once again, Adele found herself netted by the drama ofthroughbred horseracing. This time Sanfroid was third. He started from the inside. This was good, or it should have been. At the first bend he was in fifth place. Adele just wished that she was at Churchill Downs to cheer Sangfroid on. Maybe if she was closer he would be able to sense her love for him and find strength in it. She had prayed fervently the night before the race. She now said a short simple pray. "Please God, let him not fail. She wanted Sangfroid to do his best pretty much like a mother always wants her children to do their best. "C'mon boy, you got the heart of a champion.

You can do this. Adele chanted softly. She concentrated as hard as she could to transport her thoughts across the distance to her beloved Sangfroid.

A few seconds later, she saw that Anthony had leaned further forward. This was a sign that he had been holding the horse back and he was about to let him have his way.

Sangfroid gained momentum. He was fourth, third, then second. He held onto second through most of the final lap. Then he was neck and neck with the lead horse. In the last seconds, of the race you could see him striving to win. He was giving it all he had. Then he shot forward a microsecond before the finish line. As Sangfroid crossed the finish line the television cameras did an insert of Jet. He seemed very serene almost aloof

Marie—182

CHAPTER FIFTEEN

Jet was looking ahead. This was just the first of three races that he intended to win. Jet was going for the Triple Crown. He didn't want the world to know what his horse could do just yet. Adele knew that Anthony probably on the instructions of Jet had allowed Sangfroid to do just enough to win the race.

Jet maintained his serenity through the news interview, afterward. Adele hardly noticed when her father went outside and began to hunk the hom of his truck. She was vaguely aware of the cacophony of the hundreds of other horns that were being honked in St. Pierre in celebration of Sangfroid's win. She strained against the pain that the sight of Paulette Joseph hanging on to Jet's arm caused her. She was put away by it.

Adele was oblivious to her mother's scrutiny. She sprang suddenly from her seat and ran for the bathroom. She barely made it. Her heartache, and the incessant cramping proved to be too much. Everything went black.

Adele awakened to the feel of a cold compress being applied to her forehead.

A few minutes later, her mother made her lie down on her bed. "What happened?"

"I believed you fainted, baby."

When Adele looked at her mother, her mother's expression voiced the thought that Adele had not, dared not think." softly.

"How long ago, did you and Jet make love?" Her mother queried

Adele knew it would be useless to deny that she and Jet had made love. She had never lied to her mother and it would be futile to do so now. "About four weeks ago."

"Did you use any protection?"

"No." It wasn't planned. It just happened. Adele tried to explain to her mother something that she didn't understand. Jet was worldly. She had thought he would've used something. She had trusted him to do so. "Why had he put himself in such a vulnerable position? He was engaged to another woman. The only thing that made sense, was that somehow things had gone further between Adele and him than he had anticipated. Adele blamed herself for that. She had thrown herself at Jet time and time again. On that particular night Jet had lost his head and made love to her. God, she had begged him not to stop whenever he had hesitated.

"What are you going to do Adele?" Jet is obviously serious about this Paulette woman." "They're engaged."

"I see." Her mother demurred. But her eyes spoke volumes. Adele hated the sadness she was causing her mother.

"Mama, I'm sorry that I let you and Daddy down. "I guess, all I could think about was how much I loved Jet. I never really thought through the consequences of my actions." "Mama, I knew Jet was engaged and I let it happen anyway."

"Jet also, knew that he was engaged. He should have remembered that before he decided to ride bareback with you."

Adele couldn't believe the candor of her mother. She had never hard her mother speak such language.

"Mama, its not Jet's fault. Adele blushed just thinking about it. But she had to make her mother see that Jet wasn't to be blamed. "I begged him to make love to me. "Mama, Jet's only human. He's only human." For the first time Adele perceived Jet as something other than a demigod.

"It takes two." You shouldn't shoulder all the blame, baby." Jet at fault too, moreso than you." "Like father like son."

"I don't understand mother." Did you know Jet's father?

"I knew of him." You know I was born and raised in New Orleans." Adele nodded.

"You know I've often talked of my baby sister Nadine." I told you that she died young and that she had fallen for a married man. But what I never told you was that the married man was no other than Jet's father. Jacques Sr.

Jacques Trideaux got my sister pregnant than talked her into flying down to Mexico and getting abortion. They were on their way back to New Orleans when the chartered plane they were on crashed. The Trideaux money managed to keep the fact that my sister was on that plane from becoming public knowledge." And I didn't say anything because I didn't want my sister's name to be sullied in Newspapers and magazines."

"When are you going to tell Jet?"

"Never." IfI am pregnant Mama, I never intend to tell Jet." "After what I've just told you, I guess you are afraid."

No. Mama. Jet's not like his father. He's a man of honor. Out of a sense of honor, he most likely will marry me. But I don't want him like that. I don't want him to marry me out of a sense of duty." Adele couldn't hold back her tears any longer. Her shoulders heaved and tears streamed down her face. She felt her mothers gentle arms infold her.

"If that's the case, you should tell Jet as soon as possible. A child needs to know its father." It's not right or fair to the baby to keep this from Jet." Her mother admonished.

"Mama, the baby would be an embarrassment to him—a scandal." Adele held back a sob. "I can see the headlines ofthe tableauxs now. "Creole Prince Breaks Engagement to Socialite to Marry His Pregnant Stablegirl." Just like you didn't want your sister's name sullied about, I don't want my child to grow up in the aftermath of scandal. "Mama that would be unfair to a child to view itself as a mistake that his daddy made." I can't do that to my child." Her shoulders heaved with her suppressed sobs.

"Baby, you going to hurt yourself, if you keep crying so hard. Think about the baby you might be carrying. Her mother cautioned.

A few minutes later, Adele had her weeping under controlled. She dashed some cold water on her face.

"Mama, I've decided to go to New York." With the money she would receive from Notions in book royalties she would be able to make a life for herself in New York. "And Mama please don't tell Daddy. If you love him, and if you love me, you won't tell him about this. Give me time to figure something out.'

Lorraine nodded. "Your father can be a hothead for sure. If he knew, he would probably get out his shotgun. Now you talk about scandals, if your daddy finds out, it going to be one hell of a mess."

The more Adele thought about it, the more she come to realize that New York was the answer. She called Dotty Blake. Her agent was thrilled that she was coming to New York to meet her publishers. They were even supplying a hotel suite in a plush hotel on 54th Street.

"Man you sure have a lot of security surrounding this horse. "Jesus, you've got more security specialists surrounding this horse than the President has in Secret Service agents. James observed as he entered the stables at Chruchill downs. "What's going on?"

"I want to make sure that nothing happens to Sangfroid. Remember he just won the Derby and we will go to the Preakness in Maryland next month." Jet explained.

"Man, I see that you might need security, but don't you think the amount of security you have is a bit overkill.

"I would rather have too much than too little. Besides there's the problem of spying."

James was really preplexed by now. Spying?

There are people who want to find out just how fast this horse really can run so that they can lay odds and bets accordingly. "I don't want Sangfroid to be a pawn in some illegal or legal gambling activities."

"Now, I see. "You want to make sure these spys don't get anywhere near Sangfroid.

"Precisely."

"My friend Paulette has a place in Virginia were Sangfroid can continue training until the Preakness Stakes." Plus there is the added bonus of privacy.

"You must trust this Paulette chick an awful lot." James sounded a bit cynical.

"Yes, I do. Paulette is an old and trusted friend. Paulette would never do anything to harm me." Jet was adamant.

"Did I hear my name?" Paulette asked as she strutted toward them smiling broadly. She pretended that she hadn't heard what Jet had said. But she had and sharp pens of conscious were pricking her.

Jet could tell that James liked what he saw when he looked at Paulette. He made the introduction. "James this is an old friend of mine Paulette Joseph. Paulette, this is my friend and jet pilot James Talbert."

Paulette offered James her hand. Instead of shaking it, James kissed it. "I'm charmed. He said sincerely.

"My, my, aren't you dashing." Paulette smiled. She looked as if she liked what she saw as well.

"I was just telling James that we were getting ready to caravan Sangfriod to your place in Virginia." James will be flying us there shortly. Jet cut in.

"Jet, old friend, you can count on one hell of a party when we get there. Everything is being prepared as we speak."

But the party had already started on the jet. There was a flight attendant on board and when Paulette and Jet had boarded they had found champagne and hors-d'oeuvres set up for them.

"Jet, man I have to give it to you. You know how to live." James observed as he picked up a handful of the tid bits and strolled toward the cockpit.

"This was easy." Jet replied drily. He didn't looked like a man who was celebrating the win of the century. Even when he laughed or smiled melancholy still lurked in his dark eyes.

Another prick of conscious made Paulette moved uneasily in her seat. For a man that should've been on top of the world Jet seemed anything but happy. Jet was a far cry from the exurbance he had shown in New Orleans when he was with Adele at that first race.

"You never know who might show up at any party that involves Jacques Trideaux, Paulette observed to James. Douglas Wilder the former governor of Virginia had just walked in. "C'mon I'll introduce you." And she did just that.

"You know something Paulette, you're one truly nice lady." James whispered in Paulette's ear a few minutes later. Another tiny prick. What she had done to Adele hadn't been nice at all. And why had she done it?" For Jet? Adele might be out of the picture but Jet was still mooning over her like a lovesick wolf who had lost his life's mate. The thinness of Jet face and the beard gave him a wolfish appearance.

"You know they say when a wolf mates, he mates for life."

"What?" James exclaimed.

Paulette hadn't realized that she had spoken her thoughts out loud." "Nothing. I was just thinking out loud, I guess." She admitted sheepishly.

"What's wrong Paulette?" Though, we've just met I can tell that something is really eating at you."

Paulette stared at James for a moment. She wondered if she could trust him with her utmost secret. She decided that she could. After all Jet considered him a friend.

"I did something to put a wedge between Jet and Adele." Paulette couldn't bring herself to look at James.

"I see." Was all that James said.

"I want to make it right. But I'm afraid ifl tell Jet what I did, he will never forgive me." Even if there is no chance for us, at least I would like to keep his friendship."

"It won't be much of a friendship, if its not based on the truth." James reasoned.

"I lied about something. I only did it because I didn't want to see Jet taken advantage of." Despite all of his wealth and power, Jet is a kind and dear man."

"That's why you have to tell him the truth."

"I know I do. I just haven't found the nerve to do so yet."

Jet was on his headphone talking with Mr. Thiboudeaux on the caravan. As he scanned the room of party guests his eyes fell on James and Paulette. He was glad to see that Paulette and James were getting on so well together. It was a pleasant surprise. On the flight to Virginia, Paulette had gone up and joined James in the cockpit and remained in one of the four control seats for most of the flight.

Mr. Thibodeaux and the rest of the caravan were getting ready to put down for the night. Jet talked to him a few minutes longer, then he talked to his head security specialist. He was told that everything seemed to be going well and nothing out of the ordinary had occurred. He rang off and gave a deep sigh of relief. He sure didn't want anything to happen to Sangfriod. Sangfriod was important for sure. But it was because Adele loved him so much that Jet was so determined to keep him safe. Mon Dieu. If only he had been able to keep Adele safe from himself. Mr. Thibodeaux had warned him of the pitfalls of having Adele in his home. But he hadn't listen. He thought he had himself under control. That was a joke. He had been anything but in control. When he wasn't raging out of control with jealousy he had been seducing Adele. That night when he had found her locked in the cellar he had totally lost what semblance of control he possessed. He had known that her parents were on vacation and probably wouldn't be trying to get in touch with Adele for days. The thought that he had almost not came home but gone off to Hawaii for a week or so on business was too much. The idea that his precious baby could've been in that cellar for more than a week had provoked a storm of emotions. He had started kissing her and was unable to stop.

He had to find some way of getting Adele back. Could she have given herself to him the way she had if she hadn't loved him a little bit?"

That little ray of hope was what kept him going. That Adams kid had no idea who the hell he was messing with. He was not about to let him take Adele away from him without one hell of a fight.

"Governor Wilder is one charming man." Paulette told James and Jet after she had said good night to the last of the guests.

"But he's not nearly as charming as you are." James told Paulette. The two shared a warm look.

Jet was amazed by how quickly and how well James and Paulette had taken to each other.

Paulette gave James direction to one of the guest rooms. As he turned to go, James gave Paulette a long meanfullook. "Don't lose your nerve. Do the right thing." Then he swaggered toward the stairs.

"What was that all about?" Jet was curious.

Paulette didn't look at Jet when she answered. It was just reminding me of something I need to do. I just haven't found the strength to do it yet."

Jet wondered what mess Paulette had to clean up in her life. But he didn't ponder too long. After all, he had his own dragons to slay. "I'm going to call it a night." He told Paulette.

Paulette didn't mind. She was glad that Jet was retiring for the evening. She wasn't up to the talk that she knew they would have to have. "Jet I'll see you in the morning before you go, okay?"

Jet nodded.

Maybe in the morning she have the strength to tell Jet about her deceit. "You have a good nights rest. I think I'll curl up in bed with a good book. I'm not sleepy yet. She told Jet as they climbed the stairs together. How could she rest with all the guilt she was feeling?

Chapter Sixteen

Once Adele had made her decision she moved at lightening speed to get ready for New York. She was booked on a ten o'clock flight the next morning out of Baton Rouge.

It was around midnight when Adele gave up on trying to fall asleep. There was one more thing she had to do. Only God knew when she would, if ever be able to do it again. She wanted to go horseback riding one more time.

Adele eased her Corolla away from the house without turning on the lights until she had entered the highway that would take her to Fiveforks a few miles away. She had done this several times before in the past. In the past, when she couldn't sleep or she was upset about something she would go visit the stables. Jet had made sure everyone knew that she could ride the horses anytime she wanted to.

"Good evening Miss Adele. Did you come to ride or just talk to the horses this evening?" Mr. Nyuen the night watchman at the stables greeted her with a friendly smile.

"I would like to go riding. Would you please saddle up a horse for me, Mr. Nyuen?"

Mr. Nyuen nodded. "It's pretty late even for you Miss Adele."

"Now you take Mr. Jet, sometimes he will ride as late as two-o'clock in the morning." Says riding helps him to get to sleep when he's having trouble sleeping. Mr. Nyuen explained as he saddled the horse.

A short while later, Mr. Nyuen assisted Adele up onto Vanilla a pale colored Arabian that was used for riding only. Adele had ridden her often.

As Adele rode out of the stables Mr. Nyuen called after her. How long you be, Miss Adele?"

"No more than an hour, Adele called back." I'm going to take the riding trail down by the river."

"If you not back in an hour, I'll send someone to make sure you are all right." Mr. Nyuen gave his usual promise.

It was a beautiful night, there was a crescent moon and a zillion stars lit up the heavens. A soft breeze blew through Adele's loosened hair. Vanilla pretty much knew the trail. Adele didn't have to worry about guiding the horse. As Vanilla kept to the familiar trail, Adele let her thoughts take over. What was she going to do? How could she bear to leave Fiveforks, the horses and Jet? Now that she had experienced it, how was she going to spend the rest of her life without Jet's lovemaking?"

She would probably spend the rest of her life fantasizing reliving the memory of Jet's lovemaking. It would have to be enough. As Vanilla meandered down the familiar trail, Adele began to fantasize. Soon she was totally immersed and enthralled in the fantasy. The beautiful night was her inspiration. In the fantasy, Jet and she had gone horseback riding on the trail. They had stopped and tethered their horses to one of the magnolia trees that grew copiously along the trail. Jet had spread a blanket on the ground beneath a nearby magnolia tree. With the moon and the stars as their light, they had slowly undressed each other. Jet had loosen her hair and arranged it about her shoulders. His hands buried in the thick folds of her hair, he had slowly dipped his head and took possession of her lips. The kiss was wet and hungry. It frighten as well as tantalized her. As his pulled her closer, his erection hot and satiny pressed against her stomach. She moaned and her legs went weak. He freed one of his hands from her hair to keep her from falling. He moaned as he dragged his lips from hers to bury his face in her hair.

Adele's tongue ached to taste him. Her lips wandered over his jaw and chin to the strong column of his neck then she planted hot moist kisses on his chest. Her tongue did a slow drag of dance with his turgid nipples like he had done to hers.

He groaned and pulled her down onto the blanket. Then Jet was doing to her breast and nipples what she had just done to him.

They were crazed with passion. Wildly kissing and touching each other bodies. Until they couldn't bear being separate any longer.

Then Jet rolled over and positioned her on top of him. The stars and the moon were the canvas onto which they began to paint the ancient strokes of lovemaking.

Adele was so losted in the fantasy she hardly noticed the sound of Vanilla's hooves galloping across the bridge that crossed the river which led to the trail back.

During the past few years, Jet had often dreamed of making love with Adele. But something was different about this time. It seemed more real. Maybe it was because he now knew what it really felt like to make love to Adele. He was making love to his beautiful Adele. She was on top of him and her luxurious hair was a wild untamed mass of curls that the moon and the stars haloed.

Zechariah Baychan knew that his daughter had written a book. He had even read one ofthe copies that the publishers had sent to Adele. But since they weren't allowed to discuss it with anyone, it had seemed unreal. He had slept hardly a wink the night before. How could he? His baby was leaving for New York, and he didn't know when she was returning. It was because of her book. Something that didn't seem quite real to him.

He was in one of the shops at the airport buying something for his raging headache. He was waiting in line at the checkout counter behind some lady who had a hold of a whining little boy. He noticed that she was paying for a paper back novel. He wondered how in the world did she expect to be able to read with a complaining youngster straining against her hold on him. Then it hit him with the force of a freight train. She was buying Adele's book.

"Where did you get that book, mam? He asked excitedly.

"Back there." She pointed to a book shelf against a back wall. "But you better hurry there was only one left on the she!£"

He thought his heart would exploded. It was so chunked with pride. Adele his little girl was a published author. He proudly shelled out his five dollars and some change for the book. He beamed at the picture of Adele on the inside of the backcover of the book. It was one of those glamor shots where Adele had a piece offur draped about her shoulders. She looked lovely. Adele had taken the picture during her senior year for her high school yearbook. Adele was right. The secret was out. Everyone was going to know that she wrote the book. Zach was glad. He had never understood why Adele had wanted to keep it a secret in the first place.

"As fast as I put them on the shelf, they sale. It's been going on for over a week now."

"You don't say. Zach smiled at the young lady. "Have you read it?" "Sure have." She answered. "It's the best love story I read in a very long time. I can see why everybody's so excited about this book."

My daughter is the author of this book." He pointed to Adele's picture proudly. "She's on her way to New York to see her publishers about it now. "They want to make a movie of it now."

"I can believe that." The impressed girl said. "Did you say your daughter's here at the airport?

"I sure did." "Look Mr." "Baychan."

"Would you do me a favor?" The girls eyes darted about as if she was looking for a supervisor or something to pounce on her any second. Satisfied that it was okay, she reached under the counter and handed a copy of the book to him. This one is mine. I've been reading whenever I found a few minutes. "Would you please get your daughter to sign my copy for me?"

At first Zach hadn't understood. Then it hit him. "You want a autograph from my daughter?"

The girl nodded vigorously.

"I don't mind at all. I'll run right over and get it for ya."

"You seem in a mighty chipper mood for someone who has a splitting headache." Lorraine told him when he joined her and Adele in the waiting lounge. "Look what I bought." He took the book out of its bag and handed it to his wife. He radiated proudly as recognition covered her face.

"Where did you find this Zach!"

"In that little shop over there. "The girl behind the counter says it is selling like hotcakes."

"Let me see that." Adele reached for the book so fast she spilled the orange juice she had been drinking. "Dear God, that was fast." She said as she turned the book over and noted her photo. "It has been only a few days and they have these on the shelf already."

Zachariah beamed at his daughter. The gal that sold me this book sent her copy of your book over here. Can you believe it? She wants you to autograph it for her.

"You didn't daddy?' Adele shot her father a look of dismay. "Can't a daddy be proud of his little girl?" Besides everybody is gonna know now that you wrote the book anyway." I don't understand. You should be proud of what ya done."

"I agree with your father Adele." You should be proud. You are a fine writer. Lorraine wiped away a tear. I'm so proud of you, always have been and I always will be." A special look passed between Adele and her mother.

Adele searched about in her purse for a pen. She found one. It was one of those pens that wrote green and had a hundred dollar bill as it outer design. She had given Jet several of them. She signed the book, best wishes. Then she wrote Tremaine Randall boldly and decisively. She just might as well get in a little practice. She would be doing a lot of that on the book tour that the publisher insisted she do. She handed it back to her father. He made a beeline for the specialty shop.

On stiff legs, Adele walked down the corridor toward the plane door. Several times she almost turned back to run to the safety of her mother's arms. But she knew that there could be no turning back for her now. She had to go to New York. She didn't want to be in St. Pierre, she couldn't be there when Jet returned.

Somehow she got on to the plane. She had even managed to strap herself into her window seat. Adele was so nervous she felt nauseous. The only thing she had put in her stomach that morning was the cup of orange juice. Now she felt as if that was going to come back up. She took a deep breath and concentrated on keeping the juice down. The plane was speeding down the runway. She was scared. Jet wasn't there to reassure her that everything was going to be all right. She felt ill and she couldn't leave her seat.

In the past, Jet's presence had given her strength when she had to face something head on that terrified her. She would never forget her high school graduation. She was class valedictorian. With that honor came the responsibilty of delivering the valedictorian address. Adele had never spoken before a large crowd. And the few times she had spoken on church program and before her fellow class members she had been terrified. But she had stiffly and nervously gotten through the ordeal somehow. As class val she had to speak to a crowd of over one thousand people. She was sitting on the stage of the school auditorium wishing she was any where in the world but there. It was five minutes to speech time. She was terrified to the point of fainting. Then she had happen to look toward the back door hoping to flee in that direction. Jet was entering the auditorium. She couldn't believe it. He had actually came to her graduation. She hadn't seen him in about two weeks. She hadn't expected him to attend. But there he was. As usual he was looking good enough to eat. God, she couldn't mess up before Jet. Therefore, she had walked confidently to the podium. And to the surprise of her teachers and classmates she had delivered the beautiful speech that she had written confidently, and without error. Jet had that effect on her. He made her believe that she could do anything even when she was terrified.

Lorraine wiped away a tear with the back of her hand when the 747 left the ground. Her baby girl was leaving and most likely she was leaving at a time when a girl needed her mother the most.

Then, Adele's mind was filled with flashbacks ofthat morning Jet had flown her across Lake Ponchatrain in his Mirage. She would always cherish the memory of those happy minutes. He had joked with her as he expertly flew the plane. She had soon relaxed. She had known that he wouldn't let anything bad happen to her. She had felt safe with him. As she continued to remember all of the things Jet had told her about flying, she began to calm down. She let her love for Jet enfold her. She relaxed to the point of drifting off to sleep.

CHAPTER SEVENTEEN

Jet and James had sleep late into the morning. It was about ten in the morning when they joined Paulette in a continental breakfast in her dinning room. Having decided that he wasn't about to give up on Adele, Jet found that he was ravenous. However, he couldn't say the same thing for James and Paulette. They seemed to be picking at their food. Jet sensed intrigue where Paulette and James were concerned. Often James would shoot Paulette a questioning look and she would become uneasy, restless.

James had gone ahead to the airport and Jet was about to leave when Paulette approached him.

"Jet we need to talk before you leave." Jet followed her into her study.

Paulette began. "Jet as you recalled last night I told you that I was going to read a book because I was to uptight to sleep. Well, I did. I had this book that everyones been raving about. I picked it up in a bookstore a few days ago. But I had never really looked at it until last night.

Jet was begining to wonder what Paulette was leading up to. Paulette sensed his impatience. Jet if you will just bear with me a moment longer it will make sense. Well, I guess the easiest route is simply to show you." She picked up a book from the table she was standing near and she gave it to Jet. "Look at the picture of the author in the back." She told him.

It was a picture of Adele. He was holding Adele's book.

"Paulette if you are about to malign Adele for writing this book, then you are wasting your time. I already know about it. Tyler Spears, the publisher of Notions Books is a friend. He sent me excerpts from this book months ago.

"Jet you're wrong. I loved the book. After I read the book, I knew I had to tell you about what I had done." Jet the book is obviously about the love that exists between you and Adele." A love like that is very rare and it would be a sacriledge for someone to destroy that love." Jet I have a terrible confession to make to you."

A few minutes later, Jet didn't know what he wanted to do most, give Paulette a verbal lashing or simply shout for joy. Adele's note now made sense to him. But he was still afraid to believe it. "When did you tell Adele that we were engaged?" He asked.

"Like I told you, on the night ofthe ball."

It was hard for Jet to fathom. "Paulette are you sure?"

Paulette was growing impatient by now. "Jet there weren't many opportunities for me to talk with Adele. I'm positive it was the night of the ball that I showed her that card you gave me a long time ago.

"Did my mother know about this?'

"No. She had no inkling." Paulette assured him.

Jet heaved a sigh of relief. He was glad that his mother hadn't been a part of the deceit.

"Do you forgive me Jet?" Paulette queried anxiously.

Jet stared at Paulette for the longest moment. "Paulette right now, I'm so happy, I can't hold a grudge." And he meant it. All he wanted to do was get back home to St. Pierre. He wanted to go home to Adele.

All the way to the airport, Jet continued to think about what Paulette had revealed to him and what it meant. Adele had made love with him even though she thought that he was engaged to Paulette. Did she really love him that much?" And he knew in his heart of heart that the answer was yes. He grew impatient to get home. It seemed as ifthe limo was moving far to slow.

Jet could hardly wait for James to get the door of the jet open. He had called ahead and had one of the ranch hands bring his black Jag to the airport. He was bucking to see Adele. Moments later, the screech of the Jags tires against the pavement as he sped away interrupted the stillness of the airfield.

The Jag was exactly as it had been the first time he had driven onto Zachariah Baychans property. However, he couldn't say the same about the place. The metamorporsis was amazing. It was difficult to believe that the beautiful well-kept place had been a cluttered salvage yard three years earlier. What a difference. The old shabby single-wide mobile home had been replaced by a large colonial style double-wide manufactured home. A large metal warehouse that housed Zach's classic auto parts had been contructed in the back. Lorraine Baychan obviously had a green-thumb. Her flowers were extraordinary.

Jet closed his eyes for a moment and let the memory of the first time he had seen Adele wash over him. Amid the squalor, she had been a lovely anarcharism in the beautiful flowing gown. Instinctly, he had known that she was playing dress up, make believe to escape the ugliness of the salvage yard in which she lived. He who had experienced the best schools, world travel and business success beyond even his wildest dreams had been humbled by the sight of her. She had evoked feelings in him that he had thought he was incapable of feeling. She had taken hold of his heart. Even then, he think he had unconsciously vowed to improve the quality of her life. She had become his obsession. He had built the Fiveforks mansion just for her. He had poured his adoration for her into every inch of that house. Albeit, the house still wasn't grand enough to express the depth of his love for Adele. But the monstrosity of a house seemed to intimidate the wits out of Adele. The only part of it in which she seemed truly comfortable was the large kitchen. She positively adored it. That fact endeared her to him, moreso. Mon Dieu, he had not imagined that he was capable of feeling romantic love to such depths. He never imagined needing someone as much as he needed Adele to be a part of his life. Without her, nothing else meant anything. Nothing.

Lorraine Baychan had just slipped into something more comfortable than the clothes she had worn to the airport to see Adele off. Zach had gone to the plant to check on the machines. She was about to get a drink of lemon tea from the refrigerator when she hard the car drive up. She went to a window and looked out. It was Jet. He sat in the car for a few minutes.

Then he got out and he walked purposedly toward the house. She had not thought about what she would do if Jet came by the house. But one thing she knew for sure, she would not break her promise to Adele. Adele had made her promise that she would not tell Jet where she was until she said it was okay. Before Jet could knock, she opened the door. She stood back and let him enter. She wondered briefly how should she behave. The man was practically a billionaire. She pointed toward the sectional couch.

"Thank you." Jet said politely and took a seat. Jet had never felt such awkwardness. He crossed and recrossed his legs and he didn't seem to know what to do with his hands. He felt like a teenage boy who was meeting for the first time the mother of his first girlfriend. *Where the hell was Adele?* She was probably hiding out in her room or something.

'Would you like something cold to drink? I was just about to get a glass oflemon ice tea.

"Yes, thank you." At least the tea would give him something to do with his hands.

As she poured the tea into a tall glass, Lorraine found it difficult to fathom that she was about to serve tea in her home to the richest black man Ill the country. What should I do? What should I say? She wondered.

Moments later, Jet took a long sip of tea. Then he flashed an appreciative smile at Lorraine and said. "That's really good tea." I can see where Adele gets her culinary talents." He flashed her one of his most disarming smiles.

Lorraine eyed him cooly.

"Mrs. Baychan, I not going to beat around the bush. Jet crossed and recrossed his legs. "I think you know, I am here to see Adele."

Lorraine nodded over the rim of her glass of tea. All she could think about was how miserable her daughter had been when she boarded that plane to New York. And the man that now dominated the space of her livingroom was responsible for her daughters unhappiness.

"It is important that I talk to her."

"I don't see what a man in your position would have to discuss with my daughter. Lorraine voice was uncustomarily cool. Besides, Adele is not here. And if she was, she probably would not want to talk to you."

Jet ignored his deep disappointment and continued. "I know she feels that way now. But there's been a misunderstanding. I need to clarifY some matters." Jet wasn't about to get into the full details of what he had to straighten out with Adele. Mon Dieu. If he did that, then he would have to admit that he and Adele had made love. Lorraine already seemed displeased with him. He wondered if Adele had told her mother everthing. If she had, then Lorraine Baychan had every right to be angry with him. Adele thought he was engaged to Paulette and she probably had confided this to her mother. God, he couldn't wait to tell Adele the truth. But first he had to find her.

"Mrs. Baychan, I can't stress how important it is that Adele and I talk." Please tell me how I can get in contact with her." Jet's dark eyes pleaded.

Lorraine almost relented. The fact that Jet would humble himself showed the depths of his feelings for Adele. Lorraine reminded herself that he was an engaged man who had seduced her daughter.

"Look Mr. Trideaux, I am afraid I can't feel any sympathy for a man in your position. If it hadn't been for you, my daughter wouldn't have felt the need to leave St. Pierre. Now, she's off on her own and she's practically a child." Lorraine hadn't meant to sound off so. But now that she had, she was glad.

"Believe me, Mrs. Baychan, if I could just talk with Adele, I could straighten it out." I could make her see how much I love her."

Lorraine had heard enough. "Mr. Trideaux, I'm going to have to ask you to leave my home. "You have no right to speak of love to my daughter when you are engaged to another woman."

"I know that's what Adele believes. But I give you my word of honor. I am not engaged and never has been engaged to Paulette Joseph. It's all been a big misunderstanding." But I can straighten it out."

Lorraine believed him. But should she break her promise to Adele?

"Mr. Trideaux."

"Jet." Call me Jet, please."

"Well, Jet then." Adele made me promise that I would not tell you of her whereabouts until she gave me the word." I can't tell you, until I've talked to Adele. Adele will call me this evening."

"When she calls, will you tell her what I said?"

"I will." And if she gives me the go ahead, I will call and give you her number."

It was the best that he could expect under the circumstances. "You be sure to call me right away." He said as he rose to leave. "That you can count on."

Adele had barely enough time to check into her hotel before a limo arrived to take her to Notions Books. As the car was eased through the crowded streets and avenues Adele found herself craning her neck to see to the top of skyscrappers. It was a game she played to ease her nervousness. She was on her own and she was scared witless.

As she entered the impressive skyscapper on 42ᵗʰ street, Adele realized that her publisher was not a fly by night outfit. She was in the big league. Notions Books was located on the 75ᵗʰ floor. Adele had to take two elevators in order to get up to it. On the second elevator, Adele almost passed out when the thing made a sudden stop after zooming upward thirty floors in a matter of seconds. Adele was amazed and dismayed to discover that Notions Books took up the entire floor. She was feeling a bit light headed and wobbly. It took her a few minutes to find the right suite of offices.

Tyler Spears was a pleasant surprise. He was younger than she had expected. He had a lean hungry look about him, the kind that stated, I intend to make my mark in the world before I am forty. Jet and he would probably get along amicabally. And she sensed that the same stream of common decency flowed in him as well. She lost some of her initial nervousness.

"Tremaine, you are as pretty as you are talented," he greeted her and smiled happily.

Then he introduced her to the movie producer who was interested in converting her book into a movie. Adele was stunned as she recognized a name that she had seen in the movie credits of some of her recent and favorite movies.

Noticing her obvious astonishment, Tyler Spears noted, "your book is just that good."

After a few moments of inane chatter among the three participants, an adminitrative assistant laid before Adele a contract that involved Notions Books, the producer and Adele.

"It's very generous," Tyler was quick to point out. "You will receive an outright purchase fee for your screenplay.' His dark brown eyes sparkled with excitement as he quoted a large six figure amount. Furthermore, he added, you will receive a fraction of the profits made from the actual movie. If this movie is half the success I think it is going to be, you are going to be one wealthy young lady,"

Adele trusted Tyler, but she didn't want to appear unprofessional or gauche. "May I fax a copy of this contract to my lawyer and have him read it, before I sign?" Adele asked causually, as if she did this sort of thing every day.

"Sure." But get back to me as soon as possible. We need to start rolling as soon as possible," he told her. He gave Adele a warm but dismissive smile. He obviously was a very busy man.

A few minutes later Adele was at the elevator, she was contemplating faxing the copy of the contract to Lonny. Afterall, he was the only lawyer she knew. She was overcomed by a sudden wave of dizziness. She couldn't blame her dizziness on the elevator this time. She hadn't gotten on it yet. Two dizzy spells in one day. What was wrong with her? *Pregnant* . . . She had to find out for certain.

It must have been fate or a remarkable coincidence. When she got off the elevator on the 40th floor she noticed that floor consisted mostly of medical offices, and there was a gynocoglogist who took walk-in appointments.

Adele took a deep breath and walked into the medical office. Even in New York, high above the ground, the office had that familiar mediciney smell. Her senses were bombarded by the smell of antiseptic and antithesia. She felt queasy.

Adele couldn't believe how quickly it occurred. After filling out a health questionnaire, fifteen minutes later, Adele was dressed in a disposable gown and prostrate with her legs in a pair of stirrups on an examining table.

"I haven't seen a true blush in a long time, the male gynocologist noted with a chuckled.

"It was my first pelvic examination, she admitted sheepishly.

"Well, it will get less embarrassing for you," he told her. He gave her a clinical look. "According to my initial findings, I would say you are in the early stages of your first trimester, about four weeks pregnant."

"Thirty days to be exact," she said more to herself than the doctor.

The doctor gave her a prescription for vitamins and told her to drink 7up and eat crackers for the queasiness she was experiencing. And he had adviced her to relax. "That would be the best thing that she could do to lessened the nausea.

Adele had just finished purchasing her vitamins at the drugstore on the medical floor and was about to take an elevator down to the ground floor when her limo driver stepped off the elevator. He seemed very agitated and his relief at finding her was just as obvious. Adele had forgotten that the limo was waiting down on the street for her. She hurriedly explained that she had gotten sidetracked.

At that moment, Tyler Spears stepped off an elevator. He gave a great sigh of relief when he spotted Adele. "There you are." I became worried when the limo driver called up and said you hadn't come down." I thought maybe you had met with a mishap or something."

Yes, she had met with a mishap long before she came to New York—Jet, was the thought that flickered in Adele's mind. "Like Margaret Mitchell, huh?",she said the next thing that popped to mind and she hoped that it would distract Tyler from noticing that she was near a obstretrician's office.

Tyler looked perplexed.

"You know, the lady who wrote *Gone with the Wind.* She was hit by a taxi cab and killed right after she left her publisher's office after signing an agreement to make a movie of her book," Adele explained, as she slipped her vitamins into her purse.

"Oh, that Margaret Mitchell," he said, though he seemed only a little less perplexed. "I'm glad you told me that, Tremaine. I'm going to make sure that I take extra steps to look out for you." Notions Books wants to publish many more books of yours and we are not about to let anything happen to you," he smiled and gave her a protective look. Then he turned to the driver and said, "When you get her back to the hotel I want you to escort her to her suite." The driver had nodded. And a short time later he had done exactly as Tyler had instructed. He delivered Adele back safe and sound to her hotel suite.

CHAPTER EIGHTEEN

Adele faxed a note and the copies of her contract to Lonny immediately. It would probably take him sometime to properly analyze them and fax back his legal opinion.

Adele unpacked the few things she had brought and changed from the business suit into a comfortable pair of leggings and a tunic. Then she meandered about the impressive suite. It was in the traditional style, Queen Anne furnishings and all that was maintained even in the plush bathroom. Adele particularly loved the queen size bed and the large writing desk in the bedroom. In the next room, there was a large sitting area, a small dining area that was near a floor to ceiling window that gave a terrific view of the New York skyline. In addition there was an entertainment center that consisted of a music system and a large screen television. In one of the cabinets, Adele discovered a small fully stocked refrig. She had a choice of coke or 7up to drink. She chose a 7up drink. She popped a vitamin into her mouth and washed it down with the soda. She found some fancy crackers in the cabinet near the refrig. She put cheese spread on a few. After she had eaten the small meal, she felt better.

Now that she had taken stock of her living quarters and eaten, it was time for her to take stock of her life, she thought, as she pulled her feet up under her body on the couch. She was pregnant and alone. But she had a means of supporting herself and her baby once it was born. Without conscious effort, Adele's hand patted her stomach lovingly. *She was carrying a child, Jet's child.* A warm stream of joy flowed through her unchecked. How could she be anything but happy. She was going to have a baby, Jet's baby. The problem was that she had to somehow keep it hidden from Jet.

After all, she had thrown herself at him like a Scarlett 0' Hara in heat. Jet would think she had planned it, had purposely gotten herself knocked up. His mother would make sure of it. Adele could almost hear Mignon Trideaux exclaim, "Good Gracious Jet, you fell for the oldest trick in the book. You let that little stablegirl trick you into getting her pregnant!" Besides not caring to deal with Mignon's wrath, she loved Jet and she didn't want him to marry her because he felt he had too. She knew she couldn't keep Jet ignorant about her pregnancy forever. It wouldn't be fair to the child nor Jet. Jet was the type of man that would want to be a part of his child's life. She would tell him of the child after his marriage to Paulette. So that there would be no doubt that she hadn't tried to trap him into marrying her. Yes, that would be the way that she would handle it.

That way Jet could be a part of his child's life if he chose to do so, without tying himself to a woman that was unsuitable. But the problem with that plan was the way that she felt about Jet. How would she be able to see him in the future, loving him as she did and keep her distance. God, could she do it? She would have to. She didn't want the love she felt for Jet to tum in to something ugly and shameful as it surely would if she became the other woman in his life. But she would think about that later. At that moment, she felt tired, drowsy. She needed a nap. She would ponder her problem some more after her nap.

Jet was waiting for a call from Adele's mother. The phone rang, he snatched it up before the ring was finished.

"Jet, ol buddy, this is Tyler."

"Jet did his damndest to mask the disappointment he felt. "It's good to hear from you." How's the publishing business going?, he asked, studying Adeles book as he waited for Tyler to tell him what he already knew.

"Just great." That's why I called to share the good news with you." "I'm all ears. Share." Jet urged good naturedly.

"You remember, I sent you an excerpt from a new writer I was considering signing.

"I recall it." You wanted to know ifI found the content objectable because the hero in the story reminded you of me. And I told you no."

"I'm sure glad you did because I wouldn't have touched it with a ten foot pole if you had." To make a long story short, I published the book, and the sells are soaring."

"Well, I am pleased that it worked out well for you Tyler."

"That's only half of the good news." The best part of my news is that I finally got to meet the author, Tremaine Randall. She's one special lady." Jet's heart accelerated. Even though his heart was beating a maddening ryhthm in his throat, he managed to calmly ask, "Is she still in New York?"

"Of course, she's still here, Tyler replied and then added, she's here to write a screenplay for a movie version of her book." I got her a fine suite at the Hilton on 54th Street." Tyler bragged.

Straining to make his query sound casual, Jet asked, "what's the number of her suite?"

"Tyler hesitated. "Jet you're son of a gun, do you know this young woman?"

Jet hesitated for a brief moment, then answered. "Yes, I do." He took a deep breath as if to clear his thoughts and continued. "Remember a few years ago I told you that I had finally fallen in love.

"I sure do." Tyler chuckled on the other end. "You rambled on about some lovely vision an entire evening." Ol' buddy your nose was so wide-opened you were quoting poetry."

"Ignoring Tyler's obvious glee, Jet said, "Tremaine Randall is the woman I was describing.

"It can't be." No, Tyler exclaimed. "Oh my God, I'm losing my touch. I should have put two and two together a long time ago especially since Tremaine comes from St. Pierre. Isn't that where your horse ranch is?" Man now that I've met your mystery lady, you've got to tell me the whole story."

"I will tell you the entire story, another time, I promise."

"Look, ol buddy, I'm going to give you the number of her suite, and I going to hold you to that promise," Tyler said, as he rummaged about the top of his desk for the information.

"That's fair enough," Jet told him.

The instant Tyler gave Jet the number, he rang off and dialed James at his home.

"James, I know its unfair to ask so soon after you just gotten back from a trip. "But could you fly me to New York, tonight,?" Jet asked anxiously.

"No, problem. I'll do it. When do you want to leave?" James replied without hesitation.

"Now."

"There's a severe thunderstorm coming this way. Do you want to wait until it has passed through before we leave?"

Jet thought for a moment. In Lousiana, thunderstorms, especially in late spring, sometimes lasted for several hours.

"Not unless you want to," he told James.

"It's that important for you to get to New York, tonight, huh?" "Yes, it is," Jet answered without hesitation.

"Okay, I meet you at the airport in about thirty minutes. I probably will not be able to get a co-pilot on such short notice." "Don't sweat it James, I'll co-pilot for you."

After Jet hung up, he rushed upstairs and took a quick shower. He shaved for the first time in a month. Afterall, he wanted to look his best. It wasn't everyday that a man asked the woman that he loved to marry him. He chose a black suit that he'd worn to do a magazine cover. After he dressed he dabbed a little tonic in his hair and brushed it back. He smiled at his reflection. He looked younger.

When Jet headed out for his private airfield, intermitten streaks of lightening flashed across the sky; drops of rain had begun to fall and it was getting windy. When he reached the airfield a few minutes later, there was more lightening the rain was coming down pretty heavy, and the wind had picked up. A few minutes later, as they taxed down the runway, the lightening was incessant, the rain was falling in heavy white sheets and the wind gusts were up to about sixty miles and hour.

James turned to Jet who was sitting next to him in one of the co-pilot seats. "You're sure you want do this now?"

Jet thought about how much he missed Adele and wanted to see her as soon as possible. Due to a lie, they had lost precious time in which they could have been together. He didn't want to stay a second longer away from her than he had to.

"If you think you can handle it, I am sure," he said with conviction. I can, so let's do it." James said with the same conviction.

"Tell me, James said as the Jet became airborn, what's in New York that is so important that you would leave in a storm to get there."

"Adele," Jet told him.

"Oh," James demurred and smiled.

At first, Lorraine thought it was the roar of the thunder. But she went to the window to check anyway. The lightening illuminated the outline of the large jet. "Good Lord, Zach." I can't believe that anything in the world could be important enough for Jet Trideaux to leave in this kind of weather. "I wonder where he's going?"

"Rich people do crazy things," Zach commented. "They think their money makes them invincible or something."

"Well, James is just as crazy as he is for flying in this kind of weather." I pray that they get to wherever they are going safely, she said. She sat down near the phone once more. Adele had promised she would call that night. Maybe the bad weather prevented her from getting a call through. That happened quite often in St. Pierre when the weather was really bad.

Adele awakened to the sound of the phone ringing. At first she didn't know where she was. Then she remembered she was in New York. It was nighttime. The lights of the New York skyline could be seen through the glossamer panels ofthe floor length window. She had slept for hours, if it hadn't been for the phone she would still be sleeping. The fax machine made a noise that indicated that the transmission was complete. Adele turned on some more lights and went to the fax machine. The message from Lonny was short and humorous. Sign. Sign it now! It read.

She realized that she was famished. Instead of calling Lonny, she dialed room service and ordered a bowl of chicken soup and a club sandwich. After she had finished eating she tried to call her mama but couldn't get a call through for some reason. It was after eleven, New York time, she decided she might as well wait until morning before she tried agam. She was checking the movie listing when the doorbell rang. It was probably room service coming to pick up the table cart and food tray, she thought.

Adele opened the door to find Jet standing there looking as if he had stepped off the cover of a magazine. Her wayward heart skipped a beat.

"Aren't you going to ask me in?", he drawled roguishly.

Adele found it impossible to suppress the rising joy that the sight of him caused in her. In a trance, Adele found herself standing to the side to let him in. Somehow he had found her. But she had always known that the moment he decided to find her, he would. After all, he was Jacques Trideaux.

He covered the distance to the couch in a few long strides and took a seat.

Adele shook her head to clear it. "What are you doing here, Jet?"

"It's wrong for you to be here," she told him, her voice made hoarse by the pounding pulse at the back of her throat, "Why is that?", he asked serenely.

"You know, why," she told him, fighting to keep her voice calm. "No, I don't. Enlightenment me."

"Why, are you here torturing me, Jet? I told you in the letter that it was a mistake."

"Now, I want you to explain it to me, why it was a mistake that we made love. Didn't, I please you Adele?" Jet asked in a sincere tone. Mischief glimmered in his eyes.

Adele blushed. Adele couldn't answer his question. He was looking at Adele in that way that he had oflooking at her. Amusement and devilry glowed in his eyes. And as usual, Adele's heart stood still. But for the the first time, she understood what it was that had made her love him from the very beginning. It was the way that he looked at her. Sometimes amusement and laughter lurked in his eyes but joy was always present in his eyes when they fell on her. He had always looked at her thus, causing Adele to feel special. Jet made her feel special. It made her feel special to know that for some reason he was happy when he was with her. Even on the day that they'd met when she had been gawking like an idiot, he had given her that look. From that moment onward, Adele now realized, she had lived to bask in the moments when Jet bestowed one of those looks on her.

But would he still look at her so, ten years down the road, after she had allowed herself to become embroiled with him in a sordid web of deception and adultery. Adele doubted it. And the day that she looked in his eyes and found that guilt had replaced the joy in his eyes, would be the day she would die emotionally. She would not be able to bear it. Somehow, she had to find the strength to get him out of her hotel suite.

"Don't just stand there staring at me like that Adele, sit down," Jet told her. He patted a spot next to him on the sofa and gave her one of his devastatingly roguish smiles.

Adele was tempted but knew she dared not. Jet was giving her that look and it took all the resolve she had not to sit on his lap and cover his face with her kisses. She shook her head. "No," she said, her voice was almost a moan. The struggle inside of her was that great.

Jet had no right to put her through this. "Get out, she ordered, taking refuge in her rising anger.

"But I just got here." Jet cantered.

"I told you that I didn't want to have anything else to do with you and you should respect me enough to abid by my wishes."

But Jet wasn't bulging. He was still giving her that look. She could feel her resolve crumbling. She fought to get it back. "Leave, Jet. Go to Paulette your fiancee and leave me to find some peace," she ordered and marched to the door of her suite and flung it open and waited for him to leave.

To her amazment, Jet rose calmly and covered the short distance to the door and closed the door soundly. He wasn't leaving and his closeness to her made her feel weak.

He cupped Adele chins with his fingers and forced her to look in his eyes. "Paulette is not my fiancee and never has been," he told her sincerely.

Adele wanted to believe him desperately. She searched his eyes for any glimmer of a lie and found none. "But Paulette said," she sputtered. "Paulette lied."

"But the card . . ."

"It was something I did when I was drunk a long time ago. She never held me to it."

It was beginning to dawn on Adele what it all meant. "Oh, Jet this means that its okay for me to love you."

"Yes, it does," he was quick to assure her, and the laughter and love in his eyes washed over her sweet and thick like honey. Adele could barely constrain herself. She didn't want to constrain herself, anymore. It's also means that it is okay for us to make love, she told him, her voice was thickened by desire.

"Yes, it does," Jet was quick to assure her."

But Adele needed no further assurance. "Well, what are you waiting for?" She queried boldly.

Jet threw his head back and laughed outright. And in a quick effortless motion he swept her up into his arms. "Which way is the bedroom, mam?" he drawled warmly.

Adele pointed the way.

Jet placed Adele on the satin coverings of the beautiful queen sized bed. He stood back and began to take off his coat.

Impatient to feel his naked flesh, Adele positioned herself on her knees and began to help him.

"Jet, your coat is damp," she exclaimed.

"It, was raining when I left St. Pierre," he muttered, his voice made lethargic by passion.

Adele wondered for a moment just how hard had it been raining. "It's must have been pouring," she told him.

"It was, he agreed, and began to nibble on her earlobe.

Adele's breath caught in her throat. Her hands moved frantically to remove his tie; slip down his suspenders and unbotton his shirt. Her senses were bombarded with the sexy smell of him and the steamy feel of him. The remaining buttons flew off as she ripped his shirt open.

"You, make me crazy with wanting you," he groaned, then his mouth took possession of hers. There tongues met, embraced and began a familiar slow dance together. Jet moaned. His hands ached to feel her bared satiny skin. On there own volition, they slipped under Adele's tunic and caressed the soft, silky contours of her back. He unhooked her bra and her swollen breast tumbled free. He groaned into her mouth as his hands began a slow, urgent exploration of them. His mouth hungered to be where his hands were. He dragged his mouth from Adele's and lifted the tunic over her head.

Jet's undulating tongue at her breast drove Adele mad with wanting. She couldn't wait to feel him inside of her. She wiggled out of her leggings and panties. Having done that, she unhooked his slacks.

Jet stiffened and his tongue stopped its undulating little dance. He raised up so that he could look at Adele. "You're being impatient, mon petite enchantress, he told her.

Jet was looking at her in that way of his and Adele was lost in his eyes and she realized that he was reading her thoughts. She didn't care that he knew. She didn't want to wait any longer to be one with him.

"Okay, my love. My aim is to please you," Jet chuckled softly and took something in a round gold container out of the pocket of his pants.

Hold that for a second," he told her, as he gave the container to her. Then he quickly dispensed with his pants and underwear.

Adele's curiosity about the little container gave way to unabridged desire, caused by the sight of Jet's complete nudity. Adele's breathing was just as affected as Jet's. Adele noticed that his hands were a bit unsteady as he took the small container out of her hand. Compelled by curiosity, Adele watched as he took out a very expensive looking propalytic. Lamb's skin she believed it was.

"This time, I had the foresight to buy these," he explained as he slipped it on. "This will keep me from giving my baby a baby," he kidded.

Too late. Adele thought but quickly pushed the thought to the back of her mind. She would tell Jet about the baby when the time was right. But right now, he was ready and she was ready.

As Jet looked down at Adele waiting impatiently for him to take her, he thought about the storm that he came through to get to her and realized that it had been insignificant compared to the storm of passion that now raged in him.

"Open your legs," he commanded, hoarsely.

Adele obeyed. This time there wasn't any pain. He slipped easily inside of her. At first, it felt a little different than before, but when Jet began to move it felt as nature as breathing. She gave herself up to the pleasure as she became lost in the beauty in Jet's eyes.

As Adele's velvety sheath of hot pulsating flesh wrapped about him tighter than the lambs' skin condom that he was wearing, Jet felt as if he was soaring, soaring high above the clouds in a place that was suspended between heaven and earth. A life time of making love to her would not be enough. Mon Dieu, she was so tight and hot. The pleasure became unbearable. How long or how many times he had said it, he didn't know. Jet found himself, proclaiming his love to Adele.

"I love you," Jet cried with every devastating thrust until Adele's brain and soul vibrated with the sound and feel of his love. It was happening again, that sensation of mind out of body. Once more, she felt the opening of her body that allowed Jet assess to the very core of her womanhood. "Oh, Jet, I love you so much, I can't bear it," she cried as she rode the powerful spasmodic slivers of pleasure. Adele felt as she was riding the mythological horse Pegasus into the heavens.

As Adele's spastic pleasure embraced him then washed down on him, Jet realized that if he made love to her a million times the intensity of her pleasure would never fail to amaze him. He luxuriated in the feel of her pleasure until he couldn't bear it any longer. He joined her in the heavens.

After she and Jet had finished making love for the second time that evening, or morning, whatever it was by then, Adele finally asked about what had been puzzling her for sometime.

"Jet why didn't you use a condom, the first time we made love?" Jet groaned because he was half-asleep.

Adele shook him gently and repeated the question.

He was fully awake. He sat up in bed beside her. He studied her for a moment as if he was wondering if or what he should tell her.

He sighed and then answered, "I didn't use anything because I didn't have anything to use."

Adele let his answer sank in for a moment. "But I thought guys kept a supply of those things."

"Yes, they do when they are sexually active." Jet explained.

Adele let that answer sink in. Then she understood. She looked in Jet's eyes and she found the warmest smile ever. And the whole world stood still for her.

"From the day, I first met you there has been no one." Jet admitted to her.

"Oh, Jet," she cried as the tears ran unchecked down her face. Then she gave a shriek of pure joy and dived on him, knocking him back on the bed. She straddled him and began to make love to him. He was laughing and letting her have her way with him. Then he wasn't laughing anymore.

Chapter Nineteen

Adele awakened to the most beautiful smell in the world food. The scent of bacon, and sausages assaulted her senses. Her mouth watered. She was famished. She felt as if she hadn't eaten in a week.

"So you finally woke up my sleeping beauty," Jet greeted her warmly.

So she hadn't dream it all. Adele sat up, pulling the silk comforter around her nude body. Suddenly she felt shy in front of Jet. He was devastatingly sexy in a pair of type fitting Levis and no shirt.

"I ordered you breakfast, among other things," Jet informed her, his eyes fell on the silk comforter.

Adele looked down as well to discovered that the bed was completely covered with deep red and dark pink rose petals. She looked at Jet and he bestowed on her that look that she adored and couldn't get enough of "When did you find time to do all this?"

"Oh, I had plenty of time. It's almost eleven, sleepy head."

"I ordered you breakfast, but it's almost lunch time," He teased. "I ordered you an authenic Louisiana breakfast, grits and all." "You're a man after my heart," Adele teased, as she surveyed the skinless sausages and fresh fruit that accompanied the grits and scrambled eggs. When Adele attempted to feed herself, Jet took the fork from her and began to feed her.

"I intend to pamper you outrageously." He told her.

"You're crazy," she told him, lovingly tracing a fingertip across his biceps.

"Crazy about you," he countered. And you stop that, and behave yourself, or I won't give you anymore breakfast. I'll take the food away and spend the rest of the day ravishing you," he threatened playfully.

After feeding Adele everything from the breakfast car including fruit and whip cream from the tiny frig, Jet was thoughtful for a moment. Then he said, since you eat so much, I'm reconsidering whether or not I should ask you to marry me."

Adele swallowed. "What did you say?"

"Well, I've been practicing all morning, while you slept, how I was going to ask you to marry me." But after seeing how you can put away the food, I'm not sure that its such a good idea," he told her, his Creole drawl was soaked with laughter.

Adele was speechless. Maybe it was because she was holding her breath.

Jet gave an exaggerated sigh. "But since I have already bought this.. ring, I guess I might as well go ahead and ask you to marry me.," he smiled impishly. Adele, will you marry me?", he asked, his tone now serious. "Adele, had to pinch herself before she answered to make sure she wasn't dreaming." "Yes." She answered softly. She still wasn't quite sure that it wasn't all a beautiful dream from which she would soon awaken.

It the next moment, it felt a little more real to her when Jet slipped an oversized diamond on her finger. "But Jet its too big," she exclaimed, saying the first thing that popped into her head.

"You don't like the ring?" He queried softly, the familiar indulgent smile lurked at the comers of his mouth.

"I love the ring. But what ifI lose it?"

"Then I'll buy you another one just like it."

It was all too much, too overwhelming. Adele's head was reeling. She felt dizzy, then nauseous. Then she knew without a doubt, all the food she had just put down was on its way up. She gave a loud screech and pushed Jet out of the way. She jumped from the bed and made a beeline to the bathroom, not caring that she was as naked as the day she came into the world. She fell to her knees and embraced the fancy commode as if it was her best friend in the world. At that moment it was precisely that. She was violently ill for the next five minutes. She was too sick to be embarrassed that Jet was on his knees beside her trying to help by keeping her long hair out of the way.

A few minutes later, Adele gratefully let him bath her face with a cold wet towel.

"Are you okay, now?" Jet asked. "His features was clouded with concern. "Maybe the sausages were bad or something."

Adele shook her head. "The sausages were fine, so was the rest of the food. It's just me," she told him, her head was downcasted.

Jet cupped her chin and gently forced her to look at him. "Adele, are you pregnant?" He queried gently.

She nodded. She heard him sigh. Then his arms embraced her, and he said nothing. He gently rocked her in his arms.

There was a comer jacuzzi in the bathroom. The water had already been prepared, rose petals and all. Jet helped Adele into it. Then he unzipped his pants and stepped out of them. Adele giggled because he had not bothered to put on underwear. He eased his long frame down into the jacuzzi and joined Adele. He was looking at her in that way that she adored and she was happy.

A short while later, Adele began to get an inkling of how drasticaly her life was going to change. Soon after she stepped from the jacuzzi,

Adele had found herself in front of the large dressing vanity in the bedroom of her suite having her hair and makeup done by an expert cosmologist and beautician. Shortly afterward, a manicurist came up and did her nails and while that was going on a lady came over from Saxs with several dresses from which she had to choose a wedding dress. Adele chose a short sleeved white satin dress in the classic A-line style. The dress was simple elegance.

A short while later, Adele found herself beside Jet in a limo and they were being spirited to an airfield to board a charted Lemjet. His corporate jet was having extensive servicing. "Jet had mumbled something about wanting to make sure it was okay after such a hazardous take off.

The Learjet was much larger than Jet's Mirage, but smaller than his bizjet. Adele didn't mind flying, much. Jet was beside her. She was pleasantly surprised to find James already on board. There were a flight attendant and a pilot that came with the chartered jet.

Adele had no ideal where they were going. Jet had said that he wanted it to be a surprise. Where ever they were going, she knew that it was possible to have a quick wedding without a lot of redtape and hassle.

A few hours later, they arrived in Santa Domingue. Everything was ready. The paperwork and the priest was waiting for them in the small chapel. The chapel was a small white wooden building that had a prominent cross atop it. It was similiar to the small Baptist church that Adele had worshipped in her entire life. She found a small amount of comfort in that. Yet, she felt weak in the knees and her hand gripped Jet's arm as they walked down to the front of the chapel for a candlelit ceremony.

Adele got through the wedding mass easy enough. It was strange and she concentrated on following the priest's directions. Then the priest was no longer speaking in Latin but was performing the traditional marriage ceremony.

"Is there anyone here who can give just cause why these two people should not be joined in holy matrimony?"

"I can." Adele imagined Mignon Trideaux's vehement response.

"Jet I can't do this. I can't marry you." Adele sobbed. She turned and ran back down the aisle and out of the chapel. She ran toward the bluffs edge.

"Adele, please come back. Don't run. You might fall and hurt yourself, Jet yelled, running after her.

"Don't move, stand perfectly still," Jet commanded softly as he walked cautiously to her.

"I'm not going to jump, you know me better than that."

"I know." But you are upset and you could accidentally fall."

"I just needed to catch some air and I figured this would be the best place to do it." At that moment, a breeze ruffled the burgundy roses and baby's breath that Adele still glutched in front of her. "I can't marry you Jet because your mother hates me and I realize that she always will. I remind her of someone she wants to forget. "The Carribbean is so beautiful." What I have to tell you is sordid and ugly. "My mother told me a story, a story about my aunt and your father."

"I know about that also, but it doesn't matter. My father, your aunt or my mother have nothing to do with the way that we feel about each other. We love each other. That's all that matters.

"You make it sound so easy, so simple."

"It is, if you will let it be."

"I know that you love your mother, Jet. If you marry me, I will be a constant thorn in her side. Whenever she sees me she will be reminded of your father's infidelity with my aunt." I love you too much to tear your life apart like that Jet."

"For God's sake Adele, we are going to have a child." Think about our baby, not my mother."

"Jet I am thinking about our baby. "I don't won't to bring our child into an atmosphere that is filled with tension and animosity."

"Baby, trust me. I promise you. It won't be like that." "I'm afraid for us Jet, and I am afraid for our baby."

"Remember, that day you were afraid to fly in my airplane and I told you to trust me. I kept my promise. I took good care of you. Now, I am begging you to trust me enough to marry me. I promise, I won't let anyone or anybody hurt you or our child."

Adele wanted to believe. She searched Jet's eyes. In them she found sincerity and determination. She gave Jet a wobbly smile and said, "okay, let's do it."

Jet glanced up at the beautiful blue sky for a moment then his eyes locked with Adele's once more. He said, "In the presence of God, I promise to always treat you with tenderness and understanding. But most of all, I promise not to try and change you but acccept you as you are and give you room to grow to your potential.

"And I promise to do my best to always make you proud of me." "That I am, and always will be." Jet promised.

"Adele wondered how she could have ever doubted what she felt for Jet was true love." She took Jet's proffered arm and they began the walk back to the church and the beginning of their lives as husband and wife.

Printed in the United States
By Bookmasters